SENKA MARIĆ was born in Mostar, in southern Bosnia and Herzegovina, in 1972. She is a writer, poet, essayist and editor and is the author of three books of poetry and two novels: *Body Kintsugi*, published by Buybook in 2018, and *Gravitacije* ('Gravities'), published by Partizanska knjiga in 2021. In addition to this, she is also the editor-in-chief of the online literary magazine *Strane*. She has received numerous awards for her writing, including the Zija Dizdarević Short Story Prize in 2000 and 2013 and the European Knight of Poetry Prize in 2013. Her works have been translated into Spanish, Russian, German, Hungarian and Slovenian. *Body Kintsugi*, which won the prestigious Meša Selimović Prize for the best novel published in 2018 in the region of Bosnia and Herzegovina, Croatia, Serbia and Montenegro, is her first book to be translated into English.

CELIA HAWKESWORTH taught at the School of Slavonic and East European Studies, UCL, from 1971 to 2002. She began translating fiction in the 1960s and to date has published some forty titles. Recently she has been translating works by the Croatian writer Daša Drndić: *Belladonna* was a runner-up for the EBRD Literature Prize 2018, was shortlisted for the Oxford Weidenfeld Translation Prize 2018, and was awarded the Warwick Prize for Women in Translation 2018; *EEG*, published in 2018, won the Best Translated Book Award in 2020 and the AATSEEL Best Literary Translation into English Prize in 2020. Her translation of Nobel Prize-winner Ivo Andrić's *Omer Pasha Latas* won the Oxford Weidenfeld Translation Prize in 2019.

BODY KINTSUGI

Senka Marić

Translated by Celia Hawkesworth

PEIRENE

First published in 2022 by
Peirene Press Ltd
6 Trim Street
Bath BA1 1HB

First published under the original Bosnian-
language title *Kintsugi tijela* by Buybook

This translation of *Kintsugi tijela* is published by arrangement with Ampi
Margini Literary Agency and with the authorization of Senka Marić.

978-1-908670-73-1

This book is a work of fiction. Names, characters, businesses,
organizations, places and events are either the product of the author's
imagination or used fictitiously. Any resemblance to actual persons,
living or dead, events or locales is entirely coincidental.

This book has been selected to receive financial assistance from English PEN's
PEN Translates programme, supported by Arts Council England. English
PEN exists to promote literature and our understanding of it, to uphold
writers' freedoms around the world, to campaign against the persecution and
imprisonment of writers for stating their views, and to promote the friendly
cooperation of writers and the free exchange of ideas. www.englishpen.org

Designed by Orlando Lloyd
Cover illustration by Najeebah Al-Ghadban
Typeset by Tetragon, London
Printed by TJ Books, Padstow, Cornwall, UK

Kintsugi is a Japanese artistic technique where broken ceramic objects are repaired with liquid gold or platinum. Emphasizing the broken places – with the aim of highlighting rather than concealing the object's past – is close to the principle of wabi-sabi: *discovering beauty in damaged or old things. By focusing on the damage, kintsugi celebrates the unique history of each object, revitalizing it and giving it greater beauty than it had at first. Kintsugi arose out of the Japanese senses of* mottainai *(regret for what is lost) and* mushin *(acceptance of change). Some modern art experiments with this ancient technique as a way of conceptualizing the idea of loss, synthesis and improvement through destruction and rebirth.*

And who, except the gods,
can live time through forever without any pain?
Were I to tell you of the hard work done […]
what part of day's disposal did we not cry out loud?

AESCHYLUS, *Oresteia*

trans. Richmond Lattimore

When I close my weary eyelids, a pure white space opens up
in the centre is a body like a tree
from it, in places cut with a razor
stories flow
the body is in spasm, the stories relax, release their pressure
it is simple:
under the gaze the skin cracks and everything hidden pours out…

The text is like water, it overflows in circles around my busy
feet, folding over like dough; I push my hands into it, my breasts
shake, I knead it, every day I improve the recipe, adding new
     ingredients,
it smells of apples and pink velvety icing. Happiness.
Not for an instant do I forget that my body is eternal.

Summer 2014 was marked by three events.

On 17 June, just a few days after that afternoon you spent sitting on your marital bed, which the two of you hadn't shared for over a year, gazing at the emptiness of the white wall opposite you, in a silence broken only by an occasional weary word, your husband packed his clothes into two large sports bags. You had yourself brought a third from the cupboard and put into it two single sheets, a pillow, a terry cloth blanket, three small and two large towels. As you were zipping up the bag, you thought of the winter to come. You went back to the store, where you spent five minutes looking for a large plastic bag into which you stuffed a duvet. The hall was crammed with things. He began several times to say something. But he stopped when he saw you standing with your hands on your hips, breathing deeply. He managed to pick up all three bags and the plastic one. Eyes fixed on the floor, he left the apartment, hurrying down the stairs towards the taxi already waiting in the street. Afterwards you spent a long, long time sitting alone in front of that white wall, gradually realizing he hadn't left behind him a sense of emptiness, only a sense of defeat.

On 15 July your left shoulder began to hurt. Mostly at night. You couldn't sleep, so you sat on the bed and cried.

It turned out that calcium had built up in the shoulder – a spiky deposit that damaged the surrounding tissue, causing inflammation. The doctor said all you could do was take painkillers and wait for it to pass. But you hate waiting. And you hate pills. They are at odds with your need to control everything, with your inability to trust anyone enough to ask for help. You keep reducing the dose. You take half as many as prescribed. In that hot July, there was nothing in your world apart from pain. It was dust covering over time that refused to pass. You tied a scarf round your neck. You placed your left arm in it. To keep it still. To make it hurt less. All you could think of was that you were stronger than the pain. More persistent. *It will pass, and I shall remain.*

You also think a bit about how unlucky you are, how for years bad things have been piling up, one after another. They just don't stop. Maybe it's because you believe you can take it, that you're stronger? If you were to scream *Enough!* would it stop? Would that wheel crushing everything in front of it turn off the path of your life? It's night. It's hot. The children are asleep. It's the perfect time for crying. You yell: 'Enough! Enough already!' But deep inside you don't believe it. You know you can take more.

It's 26 August. It hurts a bit less. You even manage to sleep. You have to be very careful in bed. One wrong move is enough to leave you in agony. When you turn from your right to your left side, to keep your shoulder still, you take firm hold of your right armpit with your left hand. Part of your hand is then on your right breast. As your body turns to the left, slowly onto your back then towards your left hip, your hand slips back. The fingers press into your flesh, passing over your right breast. And then you feel it. There, on the side, on the edge of your breast, almost outside it. Like a pebble that's lodged itself in the top of your bathing suit.

You lower your hand. You lie on your back. You look at the ceiling. You can't feel the pain in your shoulder, just your heart in your mouth. You sit up in bed and feel yourself again. It's still there, it moves slightly under the pressure of your fingers. You take your hand away and lie on your back again. You can't close your eyes. You don't blink. Your eyes are wide open and they devour the ceiling. The house changes shape and dimensions. It folds up. It pours into your eyes. And with it the town, the surrounding mountains, the river trying to flow away from it, the sea, kilometre after kilometre of land, a whole continent folded like the casing of a hot scorched chestnut, until there's nothing but a dead, black sky.

But I must be wrong!

You get up again and probe. Your breath fills the room. It bounces off the walls. It makes the summer night day. The round lump moves away from pressure (its touch is forever etched into your fingers' memory). Panic is mud. It pours into your mouth. The night is swallowing you.

You resolve to shatter this image. Like a mirror with a stone thrown into it. Then all that remains is a dull sensation. You're not yet aware of how much has been taken away from you.

Your breathing calms. It's slow, inaudible. You say: *I'll go to sleep now. I won't think about anything.* It's easy. Your thoughts are too scattered anyway. You're somewhere above words, above sense and meaning. All you feel clearly is your skin, the border dividing you and the world. You sleep, never more fully, deeply, until the next morning, when you will discover that the little lump in your boob has repressed the pain in your shoulder.

How does the story crumbling under your tongue and refusing to take on a firm shape begin to be told?

You knew on that day, sixteen years ago, when your mother's diagnosis was confirmed, that you'd get cancer?

Or

Ever since that day, sixteen years ago, when your mother's diagnosis was confirmed, you've been convinced you'd never get cancer?

Both are equally true. The dots that accumulate side by side to contain that moment, from so many years ago, are two lines forming a perfect oval and dismembering the rectilinear logic of time. Two parallel realities, of which one truly becomes real only when it reaches its destination. You knew you would get it and you were convinced you never would. The present makes the past retrospectively true. You're imprisoned in a reality that doesn't admit it could ever have been different.

You were a sad child? That's how it seems now. You didn't lack anything, but you could never free yourself from the feeling that everything was somehow crooked, that there was something dark and heavy lurking in the shadows. And yet all that time you thought you knew you'd be happy. Because you were predestined for happiness. In a world in which happiness doesn't exist.

Is it possible to identify the dot that sliced into the flesh of time like a knife, determining the path leading you to this moment?

You're little. You're sitting under the table in Grandad's study. You don't remember whether you're hiding. You don't remember what happened before, or afterwards. You're wearing a red-and-green chequered dress and thick tights. You feel dirty. Bad. Your tights are white. There are treacherous grey marks on the feet. Your hair is brown. You don't know now whether it actually is but you think it's greasy, matted. This image overlaps with the image of a cat coming out of the darkness of the abandoned cellar. You wouldn't want to touch it. But that little girl under the table (is it really you?) longs for touch. Grandad's study is on the ground floor. The kitchen and living room are on the first floor. Everyone's always upstairs. Why are you alone downstairs? Especially as you're afraid of the Gypsy who'll come and steal you. He looks like Sandokan, but isn't in colour. He's a strange black-and-white figure who creeps into your house, hides behind the curtain at the bottom of the stairs, and waits for you. From Grandad's study you can leap out straight onto the stairs. The Gypsy Sandokan can't get you. You rush upstairs. Gran is there, in the kitchen. The pressure cooker is whistling. Pots are banging. The smell of food is heavy. You don't want to eat soup. You don't want to eat anything. Gran moves unbelievably fast, she juggles pans and plates. She's spinning around in a blue sleeveless dress. She doesn't see you. But you feel better because she's here.

In your memory, the only part of the whole house that's remained intact is the kitchen. Like a tower on top of an enchanted castle. One whole wall is windows. The light gleams. You never forget the darkness and silence raging down below, beneath it. In the light you're even dirtier.

You don't open your eyes immediately. You lie. Waiting. Thinking that everything will disappear that way. Birds are singing and it occurs to you that you're happy because it's summer and the windowpane can't separate you from the world. You get out of bed, go to the bathroom and have a lengthy shower. To start with, your hand avoids that place. You think perhaps it isn't there after all, perhaps it's all a mistake. You'll call some friends. You'll go for a coffee. You'll drink wine instead, or whisky, or cherry brandy, whatever. You'll raise a loud toast. You'll laugh at the wandering bullet that whistled past your head, missing you completely.

The lump is still there. Relentlessly present. More malleable than last night. Dancing under your wet skin.

From the wardrobe you take a lilac dress, one of your nicest, showing off your bare shoulders. It falls straight, over your lovely, firm breasts, down to your knees. You put your hair up. You put on make-up. You think you're beautiful. You look in on the sleeping children, drunk with the August heat, calmed by the gentle coolness of the early morning, and you go to your GP.

When you start talking, you realize you're talking too fast. Or not fast enough. It's as though the day is too dense to take in your words. You lower the top half of your dress.

You say nothing while he feels your breasts. He purses his lips, raises his eyebrows. He nods slowly, lowering his eyes. You feel a weight in your stomach. You ought to have been moved on from this starting point. You had counted on this spot as a place from which your life would start pouring into a recognizable current. Into a telephone invitation for a coffee that would not be a coffee. A celebration of a bullet avoided. An instant of crystal-clear awareness of everything you're doing wrong, and you'd never make the same mistakes again. You'd love those worthy of your love. You'd eat healthily. Do yoga. Be more mindful.

The doctor writes out a referral and sends you to the hospital.

There are two doctors there. One who isn't sure what he thinks about the multitude of black and white dots making an image of the inside of your breasts through the ultrasound apparatus. And the other, summoned by the first. He puts another layer of cold gel on your breasts and circles over them with the ultrasound probe. They agree that there's nothing. The second one tells you to bring your report from your regular check-up of six months earlier, which was perfectly clear, and to make an appointment for a mammogram in a year's time.

You go out into the street. Maybe you already know and your hands are shaking. You feel like crying, but you don't want to smear your mascara. You want to go on being beautiful. You tell yourself to be quiet, although there are no words in your mouth. You tell yourself: *Don't think of the worst! Don't look into the dark! Turn your back on the*

19

abyss! You get into your car and drive, although you don't know where you're headed.

Then you see him in the street. The radiologist you have been entrusting your boobs to for years now, determined to forestall the illness that ravaged your mother's body. You looked for him in the hospital corridors an hour earlier, but were told he wasn't in. Now you stop the car, in the middle of the road, in a crush of speeding cars, and run after him. You tell him that you know you're crazy, ask him to forgive you, because they said you were fine. But you already know, you feel that pebble under your skin, that sob of your flesh that's had enough of the pain you swallowed silently like a tasteless meal in a stranger's house. He smiles and tells you not to worry. He'll expect you in his clinic at three that afternoon. 'We'll go over it all. Everything will certainly be all right,' he says. You know he can't really be sure of anything he's saying. But you feel calm because he won't send you home and tell you to come back in a year's time, without giving you a further thought.

When you went in, on 15 September, he said: 'Have you really come on your own?' Four days before that, he'd done an MRI and a biopsy. It would take a couple of weeks to get the results. When he'd used the ultrasound to acquaint himself with your lump, that same day you'd chased him down the street, he'd been convinced you were fine. That it looked benign. Six months earlier there had been nothing there. *But still, because of the family anamnesis, we'll do an MRI scan and a biopsy. Don't worry. It's looking good!* He'd wait for the best time, the period between the seventh and twelfth days of your menstrual cycle, to do everything.

Four days earlier, when he'd done the scan, he'd said nothing. He didn't want to look you in the eye. He muttered that he was busy. That he didn't have time. That he'd let you know as soon as he had the result of the biopsy. You had seen him earlier going into the MRI room and looking at your reading. For a whole five minutes. Later, when he was doing the biopsy, inserting the needle with which he removed little pieces of the lump from your body (oh, what a brutally dull and final sound), you talked about your daughters who were the same age, about yoga and the summer that was coming to an end. About everything else you were silent as you breathed deeply, lying on a narrow bed, covered with a green sheet.

For the following four days you didn't think about anything. You weren't in a hurry to be scared.

On Monday morning at ten the nurse called you and asked you to come to his office at eleven. Minutes are the slowly strained excess of eternity. You dressed slowly. You put on your make-up lengthily and carefully. You fixed your hair. You put on a ring and earrings. You got into the car and drove to the hospital.

You even smiled. 'Yes, I've really come on my own.'

'We have bad news, but also good news,' he said, finally looking you in the eye.

'Let's start with the bad.' That's what you said. It wasn't courage.

'It's carcinoma.'

'OK,' you said. 'OK.'

Something in you wanted to sob, to burst into tears. But all of it together – the room on the ground floor of the city hospital, the big desk behind him with a huge computer monitor showing some twenty images of the inside of your breasts, the big black chair on which he tilted gently to the left, then a bit to the right, you on the low couch opposite holding one hand in the other in your lap, the sharp blue sky that seeped through the cracks in the blinds and the scraping of someone's soles on the linoleum in the corridor – all that seemed inadequately real, like a mistake in reality that would be put right at any moment. And everything would go back to its right place.

'But we're in time – that's the good news.'

'Good,' you said. 'Good.'

For an instant, the room tightened round your neck. Now you really thought you were going to cry. But then you realized how pointless and unnecessary that gesture would be. Superfluous. You leaned forward. You listened carefully to what he was saying. That you'd have to arrange for an operation. See a surgeon to discuss whether the whole breast should be removed or only the quadrant where the tumour is. And some lymph glands. The surgeon would decide how many. The doctor didn't say what would happen if there was a tumour in them. He talked about a good prognosis for a carcinoma discovered so early.

'This is definitely early, definitely in time.'

His words were an anchor that made it possible for reality not to dissolve.

When you were eleven your family moved out of your house into a small apartment. On the top floor of a four-storey building.

There are no windows in the entrance hall. There's a fault with the electrical installation, and for a long time – the three whole years you've been living here, it seems to you – there has been no light in the hallway. It's always dark. Even during the day. Only at night it's thicker, heavier. Like tar. Like blood. You stop in front of the building, under your windows, and call out. The door of your apartment is opened and you run up as fast as you can. You break the darkness with your body. Towards that opening at the top from which golden light gleams. Your heart thumps in your ears. You're never quick enough.

Sometimes there's no one at home. You set off several times but turn back. You take a deep breath and run. With one hand you hold on to the handrail, the other flying over the wall. Your hands shake. The handrail shakes. You trip, you fall, your shins are always bruised. Those stretched rows of concrete steps are the intestines of an enormous animal. Down below gapes the cellar, like Hades. You've been swallowed and you're running upwards, towards its mouth, for it to spit you out, for you to be saved.

It's five in the afternoon. The sky is grey and it sinks down, extinguishing the light. What little light is left reaches the ground floor. As long as you can see, you walk slowly and carefully. You tell yourself it's all fine. There's no need to be scared. You can make out your hands, the right one on the handrail, the left on the wall. You can't see your feet. They've been swallowed by the darkness.

Your little neighbour, Saša, has seen you coming in. He sits down on the ground, in the dark of the second floor. When you reach him he grabs you by your right ankle. Your shriek reverberates through the blackness. On every floor four doors open. They cut through the darkness with criss-crossing shafts of yellow light. Hatidža, the Gypsy from the first floor, runs up and brings you a glass of water and sugar. You can't stop screaming. Your hands are trembling. The glass knocks against your teeth. Hatidža strokes your hair. She leans your head on her chest. She smells of the soup bubbling on her cooker. Other voices wind around you. From the darkness you hear Saša's quiet sobbing.

This is a story about the body. Its struggle to feel whole while reality shatters it into fragments. The gash goes from the right nipple towards your back, and after five centimetres makes a gentle curve up and continues to your armpit. It's still fresh and red. 'You haven't taken that much away,' you say to the surgeon. He nods proudly. He's done a good job. He stretched the breast from above so what's missing doesn't show. You both smile in satisfaction.

That's later. While you're lying in the hospital bed, after the operation, your breasts are wrapped in large bandages. Your hand goes to feel, to guess the size of your breast, but you stop. It's early days, you don't want to know yet. And it still seems to you that this isn't really you. That it isn't really your body. That there's no tube coming out of it, attached at the other end to a plastic bottle filled with brown blood. And outside it's September and just two days earlier, when you came to the hospital, it was summer. Now there's rain on your window and wind is wildly dispersing the steam belching out of the hospital laundry on the floor below.

A few days later you're home. In the evening, when everyone's asleep, you take off the bandages and stand in front of the mirror. Your right breast is smaller. Noticeably. Before, it was the left one. Barely noticeably. In the centre of the gash is a hole. A piece of rubber pokes out of it, extracting the lymph that will gather until the inner flesh heals.

Would this image be easier or harder if it hurt?

Your reflection in the mirror has large, wide-open eyes. They tell you that the worst is over. They assure you that this beginning is in fact the end. Because time isn't real. Time is waiting. Waiting for the results that will determine the direction of the future. The lymph glands are dice thrown in a roulette game. They roll in the air. They fly and it's impossible to foresee when they will stop. Nothing is real apart from their flying and the waiting.

Your left breast is still the same. Recognizable. If you turn slightly to the right, your right one also looks unchanged. You don't feel the need to cry. You don't feel anything. You just look. *None of this is important*, you say to yourself. *This is still me. I can still be beautiful. I still am beautiful. This gash, this lazy caterpillar, isn't stronger than me.* The body refuses to submit to it. To give in and hide from a stranger's gaze.

You can't get me, you tell it. *I refuse to let you live in my body.* You rise above reality. You spread it out on a large tailor's table. You draw new outlines with chalk. You will cut out those little pieces slowly. You'll sew them together until you've sewn an image in which you are completely healthy. You've decided.

Now I'm well, completely well, you keep repeating insistently. They've taken it away. Taken it out of you. Those disruptive cells that had clustered under your skin. That mistake in the body's system. That fault in your mechanism. *Now I'm well, completely well!*

Your right arm hurts when you move it. You have to do exercises. You stand beside the wall and move your fingers up it, as if you were climbing. Your right hand stops halfway. You shouldn't, but you force it although it feels like it's going to break. The pain makes you feel sick. You shut your eyes. You persuade yourself that this arm can do anything, the rules of physics don't apply to it. The tension gives way a bit, but it's still impossible to straighten your arm.

Every few days you go to the hospital. You sit quietly on the hospital bed while the surgeon removes the bandages from your chest. He takes the piece of rubber out of the hole in the incision (you hear the sound inside, that scraping in yourself). He takes a large needle and pushes it into the hole, into the open jaws of the caterpillar. He removes the lymph collected there. You no longer have any lymph glands in your right armpit. That's why it's hard to move your arm. That's why the lymph accumulates without moving, in that place where your downfall began. He cuts off a little piece of a rubber glove and pushes it into the same hole. The sound is almost the same, it's inside you again, but this time you feel clearly that it isn't coming out. It's pressed in and echoes in your chest. None of this bothers you. It's all the same to you. In any case, you're just waiting. October is passing unwaveringly. Through the window the world is yellowing, misted with raindrops. The hands of that clock inside you that's trying to measure the time but knows only how to count the days of your waiting.

You're thirteen. You're a little girl and you know you have to behave well. Be careful how you sit. Be careful what you say. Be pretty. There are games which are no longer appropriate. Places where you don't belong. In the courtyard of your building all the boys are a lot younger than you. Apart from Imad. He's younger too, but only by a year. Two years ago, you and he were friends. But you can't be friends any longer because he's a boy and you're a girl.

Maybe that's not it. Maybe you don't know how to be a friend to Imad. Imad has sorrowful eyes, dirty jeans, a brother heading for a young offenders' institution, a mother who, somewhere along the way, as she travelled to this district where she was placed in a small apartment on the first floor, lost her proper name so people call her Bosanka, the Bosnian. It's only when it's raining that Bosanka doesn't sit on the little wall in front of the building. All the rest of the time she's there. Her legs apart. Under her skirt her white petticoat and fat trembling thighs can be seen. She leans with her elbows on her knees. Her huge breasts cover her bent body.

Imad is good. He has hunched-up shoulders, filled with horrors. Shoulders that protect his body. His body that always sways slightly, from right to left, as though wanting to escape something. He has two younger brothers and a sister. And quick, dark eyes. Eyes with which he wants always to conceal something. Shame no one has ever told him shouldn't be his. Of his mother. Of the apartment in which there's rarely a hot meal waiting for him. Of everything he doesn't have.

Haris, his brother, is different. His body is fast and upright. He refuses to accept the place where he's been put. His anger is a summer fire that devours everything in front of it. It illuminates all the false turns ahead of him, revealing all the choices that will never be offered to him.

Haris may have hit your brother. You can't quite remember. Maybe that's how it was. Your brother is five years younger than you, and because of him you forget you're a little girl and have to behave properly. You told him, yelling at the top of your voice, with full lungs, to leave your brother alone. You're pretty sure you swore as well. Haris gave you a look which said he was never going to leave anything alone. You threatened him, still more fiercely, more ferociously. Imad started to defend his younger brother. You threatened Imad as well. Drunk with a sense of freedom, flight from the rules, a magical space in which you could be whatever you wanted. Strong and wild. You don't remember whose fist flew first. You know you lashed out with everything you had, with that strength you'd later stifle in order to be everything people said you had to be. You don't know how long it lasted. Those flying fists. That body above pain that accepts all the blows and is stronger than them. At a given moment you become aware it's all stopped. All except you. Your hands are full of Imad's fair hair. His face is covered in blood. From the low wall, Bosanka is watching you with her empty gaze.

Imad lowers his head and walks away. Your parents call your name, appalled, from the fourth floor. They summon you back into the good little girl from whom you had tried to escape.

You've never before been lost for words. There have been laziness, depression, despair, a need to say nothing. But words have always been the thread with which emotion is stitched onto reality. Now they've gone. The present has been prevented from being poured into real experience. By the little lump. By the operation. By the piece of your boob removed from your body. By the sharp scalpel they cut it up with in the pathology lab, placing piece after piece on glass. Whose hand is touching you so shamelessly, so inconsiderately? Perhaps it's precisely then that those pieces of flesh stop being you. They're just an impersonal microscopic sample. It will only be days later, in the diagnosis, like a belated slap for a lapse which you don't recall, that it will be connected with you. The little lump acquires its full name, an identity with which it might even outlive you. Your mother told you that later, as long as you're alive (do they really watch over you so carefully?), they keep that chunk of you, that nodule. If there's metastasis, they go back to it. They use it to draw out the necessary conclusions, the direction of the therapy. It's the identity code of your illness.

You can't stop thinking about that piece of flesh stolen from you. That part that lives some distance from you and foretells your destiny. Yesterday morning, when you went for your dressing and the extraction of lymph, you walked through the hospital grounds to the little single-storey building housing the pathology department. You stood in front of it, a step away, in drizzle, without an umbrella, and laughed at the inscription: NO ENTRY. The most important part of you was already in there. You laughed until you began to cry. You turned away, went home and continued to wait. For four whole weeks. Twenty-eight whole days and nights of empty passing. Of time which nothing is capable of filling.

You're all just waiting. You. And your mother. And the children. They know. You tell them everything. You want them to be ready, although you assure them every day that you're going to survive. You've told them death isn't acceptable to you. They believe you.

It's night. You're lying in bed and thinking of Frida Kahlo. You envy her. She didn't need words. She spoke through her body. You imagine sticking an enormous canvas onto the wall, the length of the whole apartment, and painting it. You have a paintbrush so large you need to hold it with both hands. You dip it into a tin of red paint and slowly make thick lines. You dance. The paint runs down your arms. It isn't blood. Blood is deep inside, in your terrified veins. The canvas is covered with an unequal layer of red. You'd like to divide your body in the picture, make its fragmentariness conscious, the pain of what's no longer here. Like Frida. You don't move. You lie on your bed, your arms relaxed. You feel like crying. You sob loudly twice, then put your hand over your mouth. So the children don't hear. *So the children don't hear!* Your body is being traced onto the wall. On its chest, on the right side, there's a hole. The scar is a snake. It meanders from your armpit to your nipple. It lifts its head. Snake eyes smile. You open your own. The ceiling above you opens and lets the sky in. You know you will survive.

REPORT ON THE
HISTOPATHOLOGICAL ANALYSIS

Carcinoma ductale multicentricum (II) invasium mammae lateris dextri
Nottingham histological score 6, G2
Lymphovascular (LVI+) invasion present
Ductal carcinoma in situ (DCIS cribriform type, without comedone-
crosis, NG1/NG2) 12 mm
Lobular carcinoma in situ (LCIS) 3.5 mm
Usual lobular hyperplasia (ULH)
Lymphadenitis chronica reactiva pN=(14-/14)
AJCC TNM: pTIcN0(14-/14) MxR0

Immunohistochemical analysis in ductal component of the tumour:
ER: 95% of tumour cells positive moderate intensity
PR: 98% of tumour cells positive strong intensity
HER2/neu protein: score 3+
Ki-67 (MIB-1) present in around 20% of cells
E-cadherin (+)

Immunohistochemical analysis in lobular component of the tumour:
ER: 95% of tumour cells positive, moderate to strong intensity
PR: 95% of tumour cells positive, strong intensity
HER2/neu protein: score (0)
E-cadherin (-)

Five days ago you took the same route. Your mother and you. The Međugorje–Zagreb motorway. This time you're silent. She's brought a little cushion again so you can rest your head comfortably while she drives. The landscape doesn't change. You're following a winding line carved into the mountains. There are no towns or villages. You think the road signs must be false. They point to grey tracks that flow out of the long unbreakable line and lead nowhere. Like a child's toy. You're captives in its insides. You stop a few times. To use the toilet. Once to have a coffee and a piece of chocolate cake. One. Half. To justify sitting there. You don't feel hunger. Just faint nausea. You go through the motions mechanically. In the car you're both silent, because you yourself say nothing. She probably imagines you're thinking about everything that lies ahead of you. This time they're going to cut off both your breasts. The tests revealed another tumour. Small, invisible on the MRI, invisible to anyone other than the enormous eye of the pathologist behind the thick screen. But it's there. Now the whole boob has to go. You want the other one to go too. For the surgeon's hand to cut away from you all the places where death could be lurking.

It's nothing, you tell yourself. *They'll remove the boobs and put prostheses under the skin in their place.*

'Brave decision,' said the surgeon. The one who had already sliced into your body and taken so little away, just a small piece.

'Brave decision,' said the old doctor. The one who had been your mother's oncologist all these years.

'Brave decision,' said everyone else, unanimously.

Wouldn't it be braver to leave that flesh where it is and wait, you wanted to say but didn't.

Your oncologist says: 'Your other breast? Prostheses? Why are you talking aesthetics to me here? I'm talking to you about life!'

You feel that the thick dryness in your mouth is sand. It's smothering your words and you can't say what you mean: *They're my boobs! I can do whatever I like with them! They're my boobs that I'm ready to part with just like that. In exchange for all the years they want to deprive me of.*

And the next day you're on your way to Zagreb. You're holding a piece of paper, substitute for the piece of flesh taken from your boob, in which there were – now it's quite certain – two tumours. The round one whose shape is still pulsating painfully under your fingers. And this new one, hidden, that gleamed in the pathologist's eye like a pearl in an open shell. You're looking for a new doctor, prepared to remove both your breasts. You don't know when you decided to replace them with silicone prostheses. Probably when you first heard the diagnosis. Your practical brain assessed the situation and reparation of the damage. Two boobs are a small stake for a life. You'll put silicone prostheses in their place. It'll be as though nothing had happened. A skilfully mended hole in reality.

You're in Zagreb, in a private clinic, and you're talking to the oncologist. She tells you that the operation isn't done without real medical justification. The document that holds the secret of your cells convinces her. One of the carcinomas is lobular – it has a tendency to spread from one breast to the other. They arrange for the operation, in a week's time.

That's what you're not thinking about, now, in the car. You're thinking about M. About M, who from time to time, whenever you feel you're going to fall or stumble, appears beside you. It never goes further than wordplay. A game of bodies that never touch. M is young. Very young. You're not thinking about that either. You plunge your teeth into his neck, into his flesh, you inhale him and swallow him through the kilometres that stretch out in front of you. There's nothing apart from the long grey line, tirelessly surfacing in front of your eyes, and your bodies – your entwined bodies somewhere far off, in a time yet to come, yet to erase the present. His imagined touch to stifle your thoughts.

You've rented an apartment in Zagreb. For a week. Perhaps you'll stay for two. You don't know. You don't know anything yet. Your mother's worried about the apartment. Will it be all right. Will the bed be comfortable. Will you be able to sleep in it after you come out of hospital.

The operation will be difficult. Far more so than the one a month ago. That first one, when they removed just a third of your right boob. Now they'll take both. Your boobs. Two lovely boobs that are shapely even at forty-two. Round and firm, with large nipples curving outwards. To start with, you thought your boobs were small, not nice enough. You didn't begin to like them until this summer, when you foresaw that you were going to lose them. 'Perhaps it is a merciful stroke of fate that a feeling of elation comes over us when we're standing at the edge of the abyss,' says Christa Wolf through the mouth of Medea. Did you foresee that you were going to lose them? You took photos of them. Not of yourself topless, but – just them. A whole picture of two gently divided boobs. Not to forget them. Srđan said: 'The way you go on about them now, I'm really sorry I've never seen them.' You both laughed. You and Srđan always make fun of your boobs. Because they're small. In London, once, long ago, in the empty tunnel of an underpass, a group of lads who looked as though they belonged to a gang were coming towards you. You were frightened. But you're the one who isn't afraid of anything, so you didn't turn round and run away. As they passed, one of them grabbed your boob, as a joke, laughing. You ran all the way home and in tears called your best friend.

'A cretin in an underpass grabbed me by the boob!'

'More fool him!' said Srđan.

You love Srđan. In his eyes, life is a perfectly simple thing.

You're eight or nine. You don't remember what you looked like then, but you know you must have been about that age because you're in the room that was once Grandad's study. Your grandad died when you were five and now it's your parents' bedroom. It's small. The double bed is pushed up against the wall. There's a bedside table on the right-hand side. On the right-hand wall, beside the door, there's a wardrobe, and, behind you, a window. You don't remember whether there's anything else in the room. You do remember that the walls were pink and the bedside table white. You open the drawer and rummage through it. There are colourful pages in it. Greasy. Covered in pictures of naked women's and men's bodies. Parts of women's and men's bodies. Entwined. Connected in ways you couldn't even have imagined bodies could be connected. You feel a strange excitement and revulsion. You can't put it down. You turn the pages to see more. More. Although you're already feeling sick. You don't know what's wrong with these pictures, but you know something is. Your hands are trembling slightly. You know this has to be a secret. You quickly put it all back where it was, frightened by the warmth between your legs. By that awakened centre of yourself. You clench your fists waiting for it to pass. And you feel a bit like crying. And you run away. And then you persistently forget. Although you return to it still more persistently. To enjoy the warmth in your body and hate yourself because of it.

The operation is scheduled for seven in the evening. You and your mother spend the whole day walking round Zagreb. It's 22 October. The fine drizzle smells of winter. The apartment you've rented is on the eighth floor of a large block, which, broken in half like the letter V, greets the river of vehicles pouring into the city. The street below it is divided by tram-lines, metal furrows scratched through the asphalt. The night before, after you had got into your beds, you both listened to the night trams rattling over them, blue ones, on their way to unknown parts of the city to which the two of you will certainly never go. Early in the morning you're woken by the same sound. Clattering that makes no sense at all, until you remember where you are. You find it hard to wake up. Last night you fell asleep late. It wasn't fear that kept you awake. M had called after a long time. M, who doesn't know you're on the way to losing your boobs, the boobs he'd imagined in his hands. He dispelled your fear. You think only of his body, whose aroma you've never smelled, his skin under your fingers as you inhale it, as you drink each other in to deceive death.

You hardly feel the following day. The cold air of Zagreb penetrates your jacket and scours your skin. You're still with M in his apartment that you'll never enter. In a black dress that covers your black underwear and shows your bare knees. Your body bends. Curves in a spasm. It longs to give itself easily. Offer itself without the need for a lasting love. M's face flows down the facades of buildings. His shining eyes watch you from the shop windows. For an instant you almost feel his breath on your neck. Your knees tremble. The streets stick to one another. You break them up with your footsteps. You don't think about how hungry and thirsty you are because you're not allowed to eat or drink all day. You think only of M. His room, immersed in the soft light of the street lamp you imagine under his window, is the only point you want to reach. The destination that annihilates all the obstacles along the way.

You're in the clinic at six. Your mother is pathologically afraid of being late. You always arrive everywhere an hour early. It's only in the silence of the hospital waiting room that she feels calm. Now you too spend an hour waiting. Leafing through a newspaper and deciphering words that cannot be woven into meaning. You're missing M. He stayed outside the building, refusing to accompany you inside. There's only you and your body here. And your mother, on the seat next to yours, breathing heavily. The second hand of the wall clock moves on with unstoppable speed, but time doesn't pass.

After an hour's wait, immobile, everything starts moving rapidly. A nurse takes you to the doctor's room. You lie down, naked to the waist. With a green marker pen he draws lines all over your chest. He asks you to raise your arms, to stretch them over your head. Your right arm is not yet ready for that movement. It hurts and tenses. The threads that make up your armpit threaten to break. You feel a tear in your left eye. You tell yourself it's because of the pain. Only because of the pain of a movement which is not yet accessible to you. You get up. He takes a camera and photographs your breasts, all scribbled over. They take you upstairs, into a small room with one bed. The covers are decorated with yellow and red flowers. There's something comforting in those colours. *It's started raining again*, you think, as you look at the tiny drops sprinkling the big green tree canopies outside the window. You see cigarette smoke too. Someone, whose body you can't see, is on the next-door balcony, smoking. That forbidden freedom hurts. To sit and smoke, to watch the rain and puff everything out of yourself with the smoke. All the pain. To inhale meaning with those deep inbreaths.

They give you a blue hospital gown, a blue cap and blue canvas slippers. You change into them, sit down on your bed and wait. You think about how cold you are. And maybe, for a moment, that you're not hearing properly. You're aware there are sounds, but they don't reach you. You don't think about the children. 'This is to make sure I'll be all right,' you told them. They didn't say anything. You tried to smile. Hugs use up energy. It's hard to breathe deeply and move your body away. That's why you bowed your head, fixing your gaze on the floor, on the patterns of your carpet. Now you're not thinking of the children. You haven't the space for weakness. You don't think of M either, because you haven't the space for flight. You're here. Your legs hang down from the bed and you're cold.

They take you to the anaesthetist. She asks you questions. You make jokes in your answers. You smash your fear like a thick crystal glass in the cupboard in your childhood home. She doesn't find it amusing. She frowns as she looks at you. She doesn't want to be here. It's seven o'clock in the evening. And it's Wednesday, such a tiring day. And it's raining. And there are all those places she'd far rather be.

They take you off to the operating theatre. You lie down on the table. There are square blue tiles on the walls, like in the butcher's where you buy steak for your son on Mondays. The prick of the needle into your vein hurts. For months afterwards that vein will look like a subterranean stream gone wild, a pulled stitch under your skin. The light above you is bright. The anaesthetist and two nurses are here. The surgeon isn't here yet. You wonder whether he's smoking by the window of your new room. You think of the trepidation you felt when he was drawing on your skin and dropped his marker pen.

The nurses take hold of your hands and feet. They wrap them in bandages and tie you to the table. That immobility upsets you. You hear your heart in your ears. And you hear them talking. You don't understand their words, but you know they're not directed at you. That they're not talking about you. You're somewhere underneath their world. On the cold operating table, on which they're adjusting and arranging your body. Through your left arm you are flooded with peace.

The operation lasted five hours. You're not aware of that, of course. You're aware only of pain. You're woken by sobbing. You slowly become conscious that it's you. Your body is resisting the position it has been put in. It's incapable of moving. You're imprisoned in a world underneath the world, where your mind can't find the way to your body. They must have woken you earlier, but you don't remember. Although someone seems to have been calling your name for a long time in the distance. You try to say you're thirsty, but they won't let you drink. They don't want you to be sick. You keep asking them to give you water. A nurse brings some wet gauze and wipes it over your lips. You want to suck it, greedily. She says they'll give you more, later.

You're not able to measure time, but you know it's night. Deep night, and your mother isn't by your side. They managed to send her home. Into the empty, unfamiliar apartment below which the Zagreb trams rumble. At some point someone puts a telephone to your ear. You know what you have to say. You say in your most self-possessed voice that you're fine and nothing hurts. You're great. From the other end you hear quiet crying, which she's trying to hide. She asks whether they've put a pillow under your knees. For your mother, insisting on a pillow under the knees after an operation is a way of her establishing control. If she can't do anything, she can at least ensure you don't have backache over the coming days. For the rest of the night you ask for water. You see water in front of your eyes. Your body is floating in the shallows of the beach in that village on the coast, while the colours of the Pelješac peninsula blaze around you. The waves rock you. But this time you want a river, you don't want salt. You assure the nurse you won't be sick. They bring you a glass with a little straw in it. Before you can really draw any in, they take it away from your lips. It's only when you feel the water in your mouth that you know you're alive.

You ought to sleep, but you can't. Now you've finally opened your eyes you refuse to close them again. You feel nauseous, but you don't vomit. After your first operation you vomited for hours. The pain is dull. You want to lift your hand and touch your boobs – the prostheses pretending to be your boobs. You can't move your hand. You ask whether it's stopped raining. You ask whether it's windy. You don't remember what the nurse says. She'll spend nearly the whole night at your bedside. You'll talk. Say things you don't say to anyone. You'll tell her how you felt the pebble in your boob and that your marriage has fallen apart. You'll also tell her that you knew he was cheating on you. And that the pain was too great for you to say anything. So you said nothing. You persuaded yourself not to see. You had already begun looking for cancer in the body then. It took you nearly five years to find it. The nurse sighed audibly. You felt that she wanted to say something. But she was silent. You didn't know whether she'd fallen asleep or was crying. You almost didn't care which. You just needed to hear your voice. To know you were alive. You, in your body where pain resounded.

In the morning you'll discover that the pain you feel lying down can't be compared with the pain that accompanies movement. You have to get up and walk. They ask you to go to the toilet by yourself and brush your teeth. You're incapable of moving. The pain in your chest, on your first attempt to move the upper part of your body, takes your breath away. Your mother's already here. She helps you. She puts her arms under you and lifts you up. You don't know whether you're crying. A long-drawn-out, dull sound comes out of you. A moan that accompanies the movement of the silicone balls under your skin, on your slashed flesh.

After a few moments in a sitting position, the pain returns to the place on the scale it occupied all through the past night. Slowly, you lower yourself onto your feet. You're bent forward. Only now do you see two plastic tubes emerging from the sides of your breasts, connected to two plastic bottles at the other end. After the last operation, you learned how important it is to monitor the colour of the blood flowing out of you. When it stops flowing, you'll go home. They don't let your mother, whom you lean on as you take small, difficult steps, carry those plastic tubes. You have to carry them yourself, take both in one hand. You don't ask why. You say you look like Doctor Octopus. They don't say anything. Neither the nurse (a new one came this morning; she's not the one you spent the night with and to whom you confided your secrets) nor your mother says anything. You want to explain, but you decide to be quiet. The journey to the bathroom is long.

The pain will be relentless for the following week, as you lie in the uncomfortable bed of your Zagreb home. It will increase with every movement of your body. You'll try to trick it. Find a movement it will be late for. As you straighten up, you almost hear the stirring of the silicone prostheses inside you, a jagged sound that makes your flesh sob.

You don't remember how old you were when you got your first period. Maybe twelve.

You're in the bathroom. On your white knickers there are three dark spots. Three little dots. A strange constellation whose origin you can't at first guess. Then you remember that you know it all already. You think it must be an excess that has to come out, the departure of something that enables you to become a woman. You feel pain below your stomach. You become aware of how difficult this transformation, this turning into the body of a woman, is going to be. You can't free yourself from the feeling that there's something wrong with this blood flowing out of you.

In the cupboard you find a packet of pads, big pieces of cotton wool covered in mesh. You shove a pad into your knickers and get dressed. The touch is comforting. As though you've plugged a hole in yourself.

Later, you go for a walk with a friend. You feel unwell. You walk slowly, carefully, as though you could break with more forceful movement. It must be autumn, the streets are covered in wet fallen leaves. The pain comes unexpectedly, unannounced, like a razor cut between your legs. Your body stiffens. It comes with every movement. You sweat. You feel sick. It's a long way home. You don't know how you'll make it all that way, with that pain in your belly. The blood-filled cotton wool has stuck to the new hairs that have just emerged down there. Every step is a dragging, a pain that freezes you. Your eyes are full of tears. You try to make your steps as small as possible. You bow your head. You think everyone is looking at you. That they know your sticky, bloody secret. You don't yet know what causes that pain. You don't know whether it will ever stop. Whether it will be the same every time. You know none of that. You know only how painful it will be to be a woman.

A week after the operation you're sitting in the car, on your way home. Early that morning you went back to the clinic and the surgeon bandaged your breasts. You tried to see them, but you were lying down and he was bending over you. You could only see a bit of bruised skin. The pain was still great, and you almost didn't care any more. After that, you had to go down a lot of steps, get into the car and find a position in which you'd be able to bear the drive to Mostar while your mother, leaning forward, clutches the steering wheel. And worries about your being comfortable. And whether the wind is too strong. And whether you'll have to make a detour. And drive through the Lika district, which now, as your journey devours unforeseen hours, carries your thoughts away from your body. And that grey landscape, battered by the wind, seems to you the only place there's any sense in being at that moment. Removed from reality, from the pain and disintegration of your body.

You won't see them until you get home, two days later. In the bathroom you take off the bandages, stand in front of the mirror and cry. Your boobs are blue, swollen. Your nipples are black. He'd warned you about that. He had cut round them. There was a chance your body would reject that endeavour, refuse to reconnect the severed connections.

There are big hard scabs on them. They cover the flesh that doesn't yet know whether it wants to atrophy. And that would mean another operation. You'll watch them for a week. The left one will soon begin to turn a soft pink. The right one is critical. You'll try to find a way to help them. You've already lost enough of yourself. You're not parting with any more. Your brain is working overtime, trying to find a solution. You remember – alcohol improves the blood flow. You spend the next six days drinking. Cherry brandy. And the limoncello you brought from Italy in the summer. Red wine. And white wine. Friends troop through the house. The party lasts a week, a parade of forgetting everything that hurts, a hysterical desire to fix everything, a conviction that you're stronger than everything, the uninterrupted story of two nipples. Now in the right one as well, under the scab, you see tiny pink spots, tiny sparks of life. You know nothing can beat you.

Somewhere inside, in the quietest place in yourself, you mourn your old boobs. You don't like the new ones. These spheres that don't respect the rhythm of your body. Your girlfriends tell you your boobs are lovely: 'Just look at the way they stand up, imagine if they were like mine, sagging like this.' You want to say *Fuck you and your drooping boobs, mine were beautiful.* But you don't.

On the seventh day you get into the car and drive back to Zagreb, along that long grey road, which is becoming increasingly tiring.

You're twelve. You're living in that small apartment in the four-storey building. Dad is tired when he comes home from work. Today he's had a drink or two as well. There wasn't much to do at work, so he went to the pub. He's annoyed if there's no meat for dinner. That's almost the only thing you remember him saying, apart from: 'What happened at school?' To which you always reply, 'Nothing.' Then you're silent. That dinner with meat is cooked by Gran, who brings you up, because Mum's at work too. Mum doesn't come home for dinner. She works the whole day long. After dinner, Dad lounges in an armchair, puts his feet on the table, picks up the remote and falls asleep.

Today, you've turned up the music on the radio. You sit in the other armchair, opposite him. You ought to be studying, but you aren't. You're drawing in a big notebook. Every day, you draw him sleeping. You're fascinated by his figure, his motionless form, stretched out in that armchair, in the same pose, as the days succeed each other. Like a stuffed animal. Sometimes you think he's dead, and you're glad.

Sometimes, when you're lying in bed, you hope he won't ever come home. That he'll vanish, he and his dragging after himself, the pauses in which he tries to catch up with himself. You're never sure whether one of those times he'll just remain forever stuck. As though something mechanical had been grafted onto a living being.

Then you recognize the sound of his car approaching the building. You bury your head in the pillow and try to fall asleep as soon as possible, to not think any more. You've already mastered the skill of not thinking.

Now he tells you to turn the radio down.

'OK.'

'Turn it down!'

'OK!'

'I said turn it down!'

'I said OK!'

'Now!'

'OK!'

'Now!'

'You turn it down if you want to!'

A moment later, as those words are still falling from your lips, you're both beside the radio. You get there at the same instant. His hand comes up, moves back, gathers speed and hits you on the left cheek. As you pull your head back, the motion almost like a dance, your hand follows it too, assisted by everything you have in yourself, and with a loud thud it lands on his left cheek. Now his head flies backwards. He needs a few seconds to recover from the shock. He's tipsy. He's sleepy. His thoughts are slow. He shakes his head a bit. He scowls and bends towards you, trying to work out whether all this is really happening.

You hold up your fists in front of you.

'Never, ever, hit me again,' you say slowly, almost composed.

His eyes darken, they turn dark green. You run away. He tries to grab you. He's fast. The apartment's small and there's nowhere you can hide. By the time you'd opened the front door, he'd have caught you. You jump onto the corner of the couch, lean your back against it and kick wildly with your feet. His fists fly over you. Your legs are stronger. He can't do anything. No one can do anything to you.

For a moment he's confused. He doesn't know where you get that strength from. He doesn't know how you dare. Your feet are an indestructible, unstoppable machine. His body doubles over in pain. You leap over him. In the hall you grab your trainers and run out of the door. You run until you reach the street. It's an autumn afternoon, there's a cold wind. There's no one about. Only Bosanka, sitting on the low wall, watching you.

From early morning, women start coming to your house. You don't know them. They're all wearing long black dresses, with deep décolletés. They sing softly, their voices are a whisper, a murmur, you can't make out the words. Their lips are closed, you don't know where the sound is coming from. They settle beside each other on the couch, on chairs and on the floor. Their hair is long, loose.

It's snowing lightly outside. You remember you've left your books on the balcony. The balcony looks different. There's a sofa there now, covered in big blue cushions, and your desk. There are piles of your books everywhere. And there's a tray with broken glasses on it, stained with red wine. You go to collect the books, but your guests tell you that's not important now. You don't know which of them is speaking. Their mouths are still closed. You want to ask them who they are, why they're here. Before you manage to say anything, they reply. Unanimously. Now they do open their mouths. Those dark openings are the portals to another world. Their dresses are made of brocade. They rustle. *We've come to count your boobs*, the women say. You're afraid that if you open your mouth it may become a black hole too.

You become aware that it's night. The house no longer

has a roof. The sky is thick, and gigantic black metal jellyfish swim across it.

'I don't know whether my boobs count,' you say quietly, 'as boobs.'

It's only night above the house. On the balcony it's still day. The snowflakes turn into elderflowers. They drift down. The women say that's surely a good sign. None of them has ever dreamed of either snow or elderflowers.

Show us, they say. *So we know who we're dealing with.*

You take off your nightdress and stand in front of them in your knickers.

They like your boobs. They get up one by one, approach you and touch them. Their fingers are cold. *That's because we're dead*, they say. *That's quite normal.* Then they go back to their positions.

They start counting. *One plus one plus one plus one…* fifty times. They don't know what to do with you. How to fit you into the calculation. Is it fifty with yours, or fifty-two?

Big black drops fall over you all. Inside them are tiny violet fish. They tell you the sky is saddest when it weeps fish.

'Am I going to die?' you ask, covering your mouth with your hand, afraid the black hole will eat you up inside. 'Am I going to die?'

They start singing again. With closed mouths, as before. They come up to you. Their hands are on your body, they lift you up and take you to the bed. The bed is an enormous, deep bath. They stand around you in a circle. Their dresses sound like the sea. They take the hair off their heads. They drop their locks into the bath, over you. The hair is alive, it swims around you, caressing you. Their faces are now your mother's face. 'What's that song you're murmuring with closed lips?' you ask.

Oh, that's just an origin song, says their voice/your mother. *This is how I give birth to you again.*

The check-up is scheduled for ten in the morning. You're glad. The scabs are beginning to flake. Under them the tissue of your nipples is turning pink. You quietly celebrate a victory. You wait to enter his consulting room and tell him your perfect plan – how you saved your nipples by getting drunk. Before you can say anything, you notice that his face is not participating. He sighs deeply. You say nothing. He says there was a third. Someone else's hand had again sliced into your flesh, the cut-off breasts, looked at them through the goggle eye of a microscope and found it. A third tumour, quite small and invisible to all the machines that have up to now endeavoured to see through the darkness in you. No more than two millimetres. It's situated beside the right nipple. Now it will have to go. It and the tissue around it. They'll operate that same day, at eight in the evening. There won't be enough room to replace the prosthesis.

You don't remember what you all say then. You only know you don't want to abandon that boob. You don't want that huge cut on your flat chest. For the cancer to decide the way your body looks. Your teeth clench. You smash that spasm, you force your words to shatter it. You ask them to fit an expander, a half-empty prosthesis with a valve through which it can be gradually filled until it reaches the size of the left breast. Then the valve will be removed and the prosthesis will remain.

'It's also possible to reconstruct the nipple, afterwards, when it's all over.' He tells you that to console you. On the window behind him are blinds through which the weak November light still penetrates. The image is louder than the sound.

For the rest of the day the two of you wander around Zagreb. You go into shops. You buy two black dresses and some red boots. She buys them all for you, she chooses them, she encourages you to try them, to look at yourself in the mirror. Only then do you see that your eyes are clouded and wet. Later, you walk down long rainy streets to a shop that sells wigs. You found it on the internet. She, your mother, wants to buy you a wig. So you're ready. Ready for anything. To fill all those holes through which yet more pain could seep. You don't know what you think, what you really think about it all. Maybe part of you does believe that's how it has to be. That all of this together is how it has to be. This military preparedness. This standing to attention. This pointless anticipation of everything bad to come.

There are two shop assistants there. They're not touched by your pain or your mother's contorted face. Her eyes darkened from your sorrow. Your clenched jaw. The rigidity of your body. The assistants bring wigs. You put them on. Different versions of you, hidden under artificial hair, succeed one another in the mirror. Your mother wants you to like the wigs. She says you look lovely. That they really suit you. That they look like your own hair. It hurts her that you don't accept them, that you've given up, that you won't patch this day with locks of fake hair and say everything's going to be all right.

You go out into the street defeated. You're crying. Only then do you touch peace for an instant as you roam through the deserted streets, under the grey sky, in furious November, indifferent to your sorrow.

At seven, you're in the clinic. You sit in the waiting room for an hour. You go to his office. The marker is blue this time. Lines dance drawn round your right breast, round the black nipple under which pink life is budding.

Later, you're in the same ward. The bedding is blue and white this time. You undress. You put on a blue gown, blue slippers, a blue cap. This time you don't answer any questions. You sign a piece of paper where someone other than you has written all your answers. You're cold again. It's not raining. No one is smoking on the balcony beside the window. In the operating theatre they tie you down again. The anaesthetist struggles to find a good vein in your left arm for her thick needle. Again, the light above you is very bright. Again, the table under you is cold. Again, you want to cry. You feel that there isn't time for that. It would be a superfluous gesture.

You're having a hard time with your body that longs to be touched. You're thirteen. It's the afternoon. Mum's at work. Dad's sleeping in his armchair. Gran's washing dishes, or clothes, or ironing, or making your brother do his homework.

You shut yourself in the bedroom. You undress. You put on Mum's yellow dress with the deep décolleté. It's too big for you. It shows your naked, budding breasts. You've put on red lipstick. Your lips part. You stop that movement by biting your lower lip. You put a long necklace of green pearls round your neck. They're cold on your skin. You move the necklace. You let it catch on your excited, raised nipple. You look at your lips in the mirror. Your eyes in the mirror. Your lightly closed lids. Your eyelashes move slowly up and down. You lean forward. Behind you, a milky light comes through the half-closed blinds. You smear the lipstick over your face with your hand. Your lips tremble. You want to bite something, someone's skin, someone's body. Bite them until the blood spurts, until the fire inside you dies down. You squeeze a pillow between your legs. Sweat breaks out on the back of your neck. Your body contracts. The instant before you come to pleasure, you feel sick. You quickly take everything off. You straighten the pillow. Put it back where it was. Put the dress on its hanger. The necklace into its box. The lipstick into the washbag. You remove all traces. You run outside. To be a child again.

Your right boob is a small, closed eye. On its outside edge, under the skin, in the same place where you felt the hard swelling that changed the course of your life, there's a valve. Your hand touches it often. Sometimes in your half-sleep you imagine that the lump has come back. That all you've been through is still to come. You're becoming accustomed to the idea of your bioindestructibility. You say you're a being of the future. A bionic being. An organism that exists thanks to artificial elements. Futurism of the body. A time that's on its way. Beyond the limits of the organic. No longer quite human. No longer quite a woman.

Now you have to prepare the organism. Make it better, stronger, healthier. Ready for all the blows that are coming. Your voice keeps repeating: 'The worst is over. After three operations in a month and a half, chemotherapy will be nothing.' You swallow, you throw into yourself, everything they recommend. Dietary supplements that strengthen immunity. Herbal remedies that heal cancer. Your body resists hysterically. A child inside you screams. It won't obey. It refuses to get well under the stream of the most varied and disgusting tastes that flow incessantly through your mouth. It's had enough. Of you and your body, criss-crossed with scars. Everything seems to have cracked. You start bleeding through your vagina and rectum. You're convinced it's all over. The final end. The capitulation of your body that just wants to seep out of itself.

You go to A & E. You're received by the young doctor who checked up on you after the first operation. Your friends, visiting, said too loudly that he was good-looking. He pretended not to hear. You laughed. Now you position yourself – as he asks you – kneeling on the bed leaning forward on your elbows. Your trousers and knickers pulled down. He pushes the rubber glove with his finger in it into your anus. The pain doesn't reach you. Just shame.

A few days later, that examination is repeated. Your body hasn't after all reached the point at which it's begun to collapse from the inside. What's happened is that a mucous membrane has burst as a result of traumas to the organism. There will be regular check-ups before chemotherapy. Day after day. One small death at a time, murder by fear, which you survive despite everything. You start taking cannabis oil, in a recommended dose. A little drop three times a day, a droplet on the tip of a toothpick. Over the course of two weeks you're to increase it to the size of half a grain of rice. You do that for three days. You lie on the couch. You look at the television. You don't think anything. Every idea that tries to reach you is tiring, boring. Your whole battle has subsided. You're just a body. A weary body stretched out on the green sofa around which days and nights succeed each other. On the third night, you get up, drugged and tired. Your son asks you not to go anywhere: 'Mum, you can see how sick you are, you can hardly walk, how will you get back if you go?' You adopt a mantra: *fuckthisshit, fuckthisshit, fuckthisshit, fuck...* You get dressed, put on make-up. You go out. Among people. You talk to them. You don't care that you can see their glances, their alarm at your slowness, your laughter provoked by nothing. In that world there's nothing left apart from your decision to remain on your feet to go through everything that's coming.

The entrance to the building is under a porch. Seven steps lead up to it. You play here, you and your girlfriends. Or you sit and chat. You're usually there when your dad comes home from work. As he approaches, you stop talking. You lower your head and gaze at the ground. The steps are grey, spattered with numerous black and white spots. You don't raise your eyes, but you know he's swaying slightly, holding the handrail and leaning towards you all as you sit there on the left-hand side. You're more firmly, intensely silent. When he gets to you he stops, slowly lowers his hand onto your head and ruffles your hair. His hand is heavy. He disappears, lurching into the dark hallway behind you, leaving the sharp smell of alcohol in his wake. And you stay silent until it disperses. Usually, his body doesn't sway much. He always manages to hold himself up with just one handrail.

Only once did he hold on to both handrails. He walked more slowly, leaning to each side. Something brown trickled onto the ground out of his right trouser leg. There was a large brown stain on his backside. The stench of the alcohol mixed with the stench of what you didn't want to know. Then your friends also looked at the ground. Your shame flooded through them.

The light is yellow. The doorbell rings. Your son had gone to buy chocolate and now he's home. As you open the door for him, you think how yellow the light in your house is. It's raining outside. He's behind you. The house in front of you stands empty. The big living room with the kitchen and dining room, the open doors of the bedrooms. The house opens itself up to you, quiet and tranquil. As though it wants you to remember it, in that yellowness which is being destroyed by the grey coming through the windows. Is there any point in remembering, just at this moment? There's something wrong with this line of thinking. Your memory is unnecessary. Can it remember you, that's the question. In your skinny jeans and big, baggy cotton top? Your hair has just been washed, it falls onto your shoulders. You still have hair. The wig is in a box (it arrived by post, a gift from a friend). You're ready. Although you don't want to wear it. Not all the time, no way. Just sometimes. (Perhaps when you go to see M.) It's white. Completely unnatural. That was the only condition. Your wig had to look unnatural. Like a wig. Yes, a wig. *This thing on my head is a wig!* So no one will think you're hiding behind someone else's hair. So no one will think you aren't strong. It doesn't matter who they are. As long as they play their role according to the rules – a witness who confirms your existence. Looks at you. You're fighting. You're winning. You can do anything. You, against everyone.

You'd like to light up. Draw the smoke deep into yourself. You don't. Perhaps more for their sake than yours. Isn't that the stupidest, most senseless thing in the world, to have cancer and smoke? You don't feel that fear. You feel only the gaze of someone else who's going to judge you.

Somewhere deep, deep inside you is calm. You stand upright. Your body sways slightly. You don't hear the din, the clamour that wants to drive you to panic. You're not afraid. Your eyes are wide open. You don't look away from the mirror. You want to delve into what you see inside. Is this death, this dark circle that refuses to give way before your gaze? The watery pupil devouring your eye.

Now, in the face of this empty house, you don't feel anything as you hear your son's footsteps behind you. Should you cry? Wonder what he'd do if you…? You don't feel anything. Maybe that's the place that remains after pain, after fear.

At this point he enters the whole story. A man. A lover. A real person, who will try to save you. He succeeds in holding you still. He doesn't fly past you like everything else, with the speed of road signs beside the motorway. You love his lips. His teeth when he laughs. Your shared silence. In the quiet of his car, words are redundant. You're beautiful, here, in his eyes.

'You'll be beautiful even when you're bald,' he says.

'Even when my eyebrows and eyelashes fall off?' you ask out loud, to show that this doesn't hurt you.

'Even then. You'll always be beautiful.' He smiles. Maybe you even believe him, in that moment. Maybe later too.

Some other night, in the dense darkness of your room, you draw those sentences out of you, turn them round, stick them onto yourself until you begin to cry.

Now he's holding your hand in his, taking it to his lips and kissing it. His lips are soft. His lips are caramel covered in milk, which your grandmother made for you when you were little and had a sore throat. You've bought two bottles of cider. Earlier, in a cafe, with some other people, you drank red wine. You pretended you didn't know that just a couple of hours later you'd be sitting in his car. In silence. Breathing rapidly. It's December. It's cold. The streets are narrow and deserted. You talk a bit about going for another drink. You know you won't.

'It's late,' he says, slowly turning the steering wheel. 'I don't know what's open any more. Can we just sit in the car for a while?'

'Yes,' you say softly. 'We can.'

The streets merge into one another. You're going along a route you'll be repeating the very next morning, your stomach clenched. *It's nothing, I can do it, I'm strong.* You stop in a big car park. In the dark. The whole world is in the dark. The only light comes from the windows of the round, red, odd-looking oncology building opposite. You say nothing. At this moment, it's the only place where there's any point in being. You think this building is a crash-landed UFO. There are panicking aliens inside it. They run behind those dazzling windows trying to find a means of escape. You're convinced he's thinking the same thing. That this place can't be real.

Afterwards, you kiss. Until your teeth start hurting. Your hair is dancing. You open your eyes. His hand is on your bare legs. They look white in the darkness, destroying and annihilating everything around the two of you. The surreality of this image heals you the following morning. You park in the same place. You get out of the car and go for your first chemotherapy session.

You're only four. You're playing in the courtyard in front of the building. You're wearing a little red dress scattered with tiny white hearts. You're playing hopscotch. You jump on one leg. Hopping from one square to another. You look at your foot, in a little white sock and a black patent leather shoe. You enjoy the leap from the ground, the brief flight, the air that touches your bare knees. It's not enough. It doesn't last long. You want more. You jump over two squares at a time. Your body is a bird's body. Light. You want more. The flying never to stop. The space of freedom between landings. So you leap up to jump three squares. Your foot twists as you land, and you fall head first. The blow of your forehead echoes on the asphalt.

Your friends take you up to the apartment, where your family will live for just six months before returning, repentant, to your grandmother's house. They hold you under your arms, dragging you. Your head flops. You see small drops of blood. They fall onto the steps. Every few steps a drop, red, round, on the grey concrete. They ring the doorbell.

Your father opens the door. He's angry. Only briefly. He's angry because he had to get up, to let someone into his afternoon. The next moment, his face expresses only fear. He doesn't know what to do with you in this state. You feel

74

that clearly. Mum isn't at home. It's just the two of you. He takes you and lays you down on the sofa in the living room. He stands over you and doesn't know what to do. You feel his confusion. You feel you're in the way, that you're a nuisance, that he isn't ready to deal with you. He's brought a wet cloth and laid it on your forehead. You don't stir. Your eyes are open. You see your feet, you've still got your shoes on. Behind the sofa is a door. Beside the door, on the wall, there's a clock, you know that, but you don't know what time it is. You lie there. In your memory, that afternoon has no sound. You sense you have come to the end. Death is a big black mouth, coming towards you to swallow you up. He stands beside you and can't think of words to comfort you. You don't know whether you're crying.

(AC)

Adjuvant chemotherapy (AC) is recommended in the treatment of patients with HER2-positive tumours, triply negative tumours and patients with HER2-positive lymph nodes. In the group of ER-positive and HER2-negative patients, bearing in mind the benefit/damage of AC, the decision to use AC should be made on the basis of other risk factors. Anthracycline protocols (FEC, FAC 6 cycle) can be administered to all patients and is particularly recommended for HER2-positive patients. Before prescribing anthracycline, an ultrasound of the heart should be carried out with left ventricular ejection fraction. Taxanes (AC-T protocol) are recommended for high-risk patients. High-dose density protocol – AC-T protocol (AC fortnightly and T at weekly intervals) is recommended for young patients. Anthracycline protocols (CMF) may be given to older patients and patients with cardiac dysfunction.

There are six beds and eight chairs in the room. You've dressed nicely. Put on make-up. You're determined to go through it all with a smile. Which wore a little thin during the two hours you spent in the waiting room. Then you were summoned to the intern. Then to the doctor. Then they weighed you. Finally, you're in this room. Your eyes are wide and you drink in this world. Your breath is rapid and shallow. You keep hold of that now weary smile. Most of the beds and chairs are occupied. From them, empty, indifferent eyes look out at you from bald heads, covered in caps, scarves or wigs. You think: *Those poor, poor, sick people*. As though you're not one of them. Your smile is a spasm that's beginning to hurt.

You won't be smiling like that for long.

I will, I'll smile the whole time.

Well, we'll see.

Yes, you'll see.

You say all that through your glances. They're saying it to make it easier for you. You insist that it's not necessary, that you're stronger.

You have to lie down. You can't do it sitting up. The nurses try to be cheerful. There are five of them. You all laugh out loud. There's a little party going on around your bed. A First

77

Chemotherapy party. On the bed, beside your legs, they've laid a dozen syringes.

Olivera takes your left arm. Nothing can go into your right arm because of the extracted lymph nodes. They look for a vein. Your veins are still relatively good. First they insert a cannula. They explain everything they're going to do. They tell you the order. Premedication. Then a bag of physiological solution. AC chemotherapy. Physiological again. That's it. The first of four AC sessions, one every three weeks. After that there will be twelve Taxols, one a week. AC + T. Standard protocol. There's nothing special about you.

AC is a red fluid. Afterwards, you won't be able to stand the colour red. The AC is in a bag. A nurse brought it in, wearing rubber gloves. She hooked it to a stand beside your bed. The red drops trickle down the plastic tube. They enter your arm slowly. You shouldn't feel anything, but there's a vague displacement here, as though part of you is emerging from your body, just a centimetre, almost imperceptibly, crossing over its edge. The dripping in of the drug lasts around an hour and a half, maybe more.

You've opened a book and you're reading. The letters dance before your eyes, the words make no sense, the sentences suffocate you, overtake one another. You don't give up. Words, even without meaning, are your home, you use them to eradicate fear.

When you get home, you'll wait for the side effects to start, determined that you're stronger. *I won't feel it*, you tell yourself. You have to keep your body moving. You need to drink a lot of water, to wash that redness out of you. You fill a large mineral water bottle with tap water so you can measure the quantity and pour it into yourself. You call your friends and tell them how well you are. That you can't feel anything. You don't tell them about your fear. It's not included in the relevant symptoms of that day. You take a mat, lay it on the floor and do yoga for the next hour. You stretch your body. You convince it that it's stronger than everything. A bag of red fluid can't compete with its strength.

You finish your yoga practice at seven in the evening. Then it begins. Like an unexpected blow to the stomach. The floor shifts under your feet.

The nausea began that same night. The tablets they'd given you didn't help. The world swayed. Colours dissolved. Reality crumbled.

Your stomach churns, it wants to escape from your body. You know you're in the living room, in your own home. Your furniture's here. The windows with your view. The sofa is still green. The kitchen white. Everything's in the right place, only your eyes are losing focus. Your innards seem to want to get out. Your body wants to turn itself inside out. To breathe. You keep your eyes open, so as not to sink, but you slide into the depths. You occupy two worlds at the same time. The world of your home, with its familiar outlines and smell. The space through which your children pass, your mother urging you to eat, although you can't open your mouth. And a world which is like a drawing on transparent film thrown over the real world.

Here, the only colours are black and red. You're lost in a vast hotel. However hard you try, you can't count the floors. Some of them don't have external walls, only an inside, while outside it's dark. You're looking for your room. It's number 303, you know that. For some reason, that's the only thing you know.

For the next four days, in that world on top of the world, in that red and black chaos, you try to find your room. The corridors are full of people with various parts of their bodies missing. You can hardly squeeze through the throng. You hardly manage to say a word in conversation with your daughter, who's now sitting beside you, on this green sofa. You're tired, from forging a path through those bodies. From searching for that room, in which you only want to use the bathroom, to soothe your body under a stream of warm water.

The rooms move away from you. Those people start resembling cells that are dividing too rapidly. You can hardly breathe. You push. You make your way through them. For four days. While you're awake and while you sleep, you're looking for the way out.

Two weeks after the chemotherapy, your hair began to fall out. It became stiff, alien, dead, then it started sliding off your head, sharp and heavy. A month earlier, you had a pageboy cut.

The roots hurt. This pain is irrelevant; so many other things have already hurt you.

It's now 31 December. You go to the hairdresser again. Other women are sitting under dryers, getting ready for the New Year festivities. Your hair falls out, onto the floor. On your head it's short, cut to one centimetre.

By evening, still more will start falling out. You put on a hat. You'll bear it for another two days, that departure of yourself from yourself, your disintegration. Then you shut yourself in the bathroom. You call the children. You tell them it'll be fun. You'll have a balding celebration. Celebrating a smooth skull. Celebrating the speeding up of a lengthy depilation. They don't think it's funny. They don't want to join you, to be participants in yet another step of your transformation, on the path to unrecognizability.

You take the little electric razor. You pass it over your head. With every tuft that falls, you give yourself back one lost, stolen part of yourself. You pick up a large men's razor, with five blades. You run it over your head, hidden under a thick layer of shaving foam. You don't think anything. This bald head is your choice. You're free. You put on make-up. You put on big earrings. You look at yourself in the mirror. You think how lovely you look.

Fuck cancer! That's what you tell it.

For sores in the vaginal area of the body, fill a bath ¼ full of warm water. Sprinkle sea salt into the water, in sufficient quantity to make the water taste salty. Sit in the bath, with the knees touching the chest or legs open over the edge of the bath. Stay in the bath for at least twenty minutes. Twice a day.

You prefer the first variant. That way you don't have to lean your back against the cold bath. So at first glance at least it looks like a pose you have chosen yourself, deliberately and gladly. That you want to sit here.

Twice twenty minutes is forty minutes. Forty minutes sitting in the bath, in shallow water. You hug your bare legs. You rest your head on your knees. You think it doesn't matter. That it's not insupportable. That through your sunken rump the last drops of the secret are seeping out of your body.

Another eight minutes, and that's it! Don't think! It's just one of the things you have to do. Be happy! It doesn't hurt when you use the toilet! What if it did? What if it did? Imagine how you'd feel then? Imagine! Be happy!

To make the best use of the time, those twice twenty minutes, why don't you treat the wounds in your mouth at the same time? You take a bottle of water with salt and soda sprinkled into it. You fill your mouth and swish it around. *Maybe I'm becoming a fish!* you think. *All that salt and water.*

But it only covers your legs and fills your mouth. *Maybe I'm becoming a mermaid! A real mermaid!* Instead of legs you'll have a tail, silver scales that glow in the dark. You'll sing in the voice of a mermaid. Wreck ships. Drive sailors mad with the flicking of your perfect body. You – eternal. You – a fish-woman. With your rump sunk in fifteen centimetres of salt water, you're ready for your metamorphosis.

After two days, you want to stop. The sores still hurt. You're afraid of how it will be if they spread. You find it hard to accept the idea that your mucous membrane could rupture just like that. By itself. A quiet implosion. Invisible chemochemical drops circulate through your body, slowly destroying it. *Don't think about that! Think about how it's curing you! How it's helping you! Be happy!*

You can't stand the silence of the bathroom. Your vague outline in the glass of the shower cubicle. A white bent body without a single hair. That's why you now pour that salty bath into a large round tub. You put it on the step that divides the living room from the kitchen. The step that's opposite the television which you intend to stare at, to kill the time, the minutes which, like tar, dissolve slowly and mercilessly. You take the clothes off your lower body. You tell the children not to come into the living room. You wrap a blanket around your shoulders and lower yourself into the tub.

But you forgot to include mass in that equation. The water overflows. It pours down the steps. It flows over the parquet. You're stuck. There's nothing for it but to call the children. One holds on to the basin, the other on to you. They pull you out. They bring towels and throw them onto the floor. Your living room is a beach that's been surprised by waves. Brightly coloured, pretty and wet. You all laugh. With laughter, like a pressure cooker whistling, you all drive out your fear.

Food is your enemy. A necessary evil which you resist. The smell is heavy, the textures never sufficiently bearable for your palette. Gran always worries about this. That you don't eat. You don't eat anything. How thin you are. Skin and bones. And little anyway. 'A sorry sight,' she once said, thinking you couldn't hear. You thought you'd never grow. You'd always be the same, small, stunted, skinny, a sorry sight. That makes your stomach hurt. Almost every day. Clenched in pain. And you can't go to the toilet.

'Her stool's baked because she doesn't eat anything,' she said.

That word haunts you. The fear that your insides are abandoned black ashes. That makes it even harder to open your mouth, to swallow a mouthful. The cottage cheese is hard, just out of the fridge, spread in lumps on a slice of bread. She presses it with her fingers to thaw it, so it spreads. You can't force yourself to open your mouth.

The pains in your stomach mean you can't straighten your legs when things are hard or when you're frightened. Sometimes your friends take you home from school, so bad is that pain. That howl inside you. Your body is bent double. Rigid.

You sit down to lunch. You struggle to bring your fork to your mouth. You feel Gran's anxiety. Mum's anxiety. Dad's anger. The silence is dense. From time to time Gran or Mum will say: 'You have to' or 'Just a little' or 'Just two more mouthfuls' or 'You like it?' Your stomach clenches because you know it's all your fault. If you could be good, if you'd eat up everything in front of you, everything at this table would be different, nicer. You wouldn't all be stifled by this bloated silence. Definitely.

Dad thinks soup is the most important thing.

'If you don't eat it,' Gran says, 'I'll tell Daddy.' But she doesn't.

Once she really did tell him. He sat you down at the kitchen table. In front of the pink wall where two coloured decorative plates hung. He put soup in front of you, yellowish water with some noodles and little pieces of carrot scattered in it. He broke bread into little pieces and crumbled them into it.

You looked at the sodden bread in that water, at the pink wall in front of you. He pushed a spoon into your mouth. You clenched your teeth. The soup ran down your chin. Your stomach rose as you swallowed. He yelled. You don't remember what, but he certainly shouted. You cried, you know that for sure, all that salt couldn't have been from the soup alone. And then, like a rising tide, you started to vomit. A stream sputtered out of your mouth. Salty water with sodden pieces of bread and carrot went back into the bowl, overflowing onto the table.

He said nothing and watched you. You had won.

In the time between the first and second treatments, they took three blood samples. The second time was on the day before the date scheduled for the second treatment.

The levels of neutrophils and leucocytes weren't good. The treatment was postponed for three days. For three days you were haunted by the fear that it would be too late. That your white blood cells would forever refuse to participate in your recovery. You'd never be able to take the second dose. You'd never be able to breathe normally again, without a spasm. The fear that some new, fourth intruder had begun to prowl through your body suffocated you. It was lurking in the places where you were weakest, those pockets where your strength betrayed you, without the red fluid that, coursing through your veins, killed everything in its path.

Three days later, the results were good enough. But your veins were beginning to be problematic. Frightened. Hidden.

It's January. It's cold. People cough and sneeze. Your mother is pathologically afraid you're going to *get ill*. That some pointless virus will finish you off. When you go for blood tests, you wear a mask over your mouth and nose. At your approach, bald, made-up, with big earrings, in the nicest outfit you possess, with a mask over your face, people part like river water trying to get out of its bed. You're always first. Barely concealed pitying looks pass over you. And so, although it's cold, you don't wear a hat. You don't wear your wig either (it's still in the box it came in). You parade your bald head, white and weary, like a flag. That's how you say you're stronger than everything, that there's no price you won't pay to remain.

At the second treatment, they reduce the dose, the number of units they inject into your body. They hope you'll take it better that way. They prick you three times before they find a vein that gives way. You tell your insides to let go, to surrender. Open up to the bag of red fluid. Let it pour into you. Now you believe again, now you are resolute again that you'll get through it all on your own two feet. You'll be stronger than the nausea, than the images that dim your gaze. All that exists are you and the red liquid in your veins. *I'll win this time*, you tell it. *You won't knock me down.*

That day, in the corridor, during your two-hour wait in the oncology department, you run into Aida. You went to secondary school together. You didn't know she was ill. She didn't know about you either. She too is having her second treatment. You can see black hair under the scarf tied round her head. 'How come you've got hair?' you ask her. You both laugh.

For a moment you may have thought of telling each other how you each felt after the first treatment. But you both know it can't be expressed.

Her body is stiff. Belligerent and determined, she holds her fists clenched. Something your eye can't see is attacking her. She's on her guard, ready to respond. You think that all the energy with which she's holding her body rigid is spilling out into a nothingness where every movement is excessive. You wonder whether you look like that too. Is your laughter equally false, your strength so brittle?

She's going to stay in the hospital for three days. That's how long it takes for her treatment. Her cancer is in the womb. Yours only takes an hour. *How lucky I am*, you think. *How lucky, just one hour.*

The women visit you again, at night. This time they come one by one. They make their way into your room through the mirror and sit down on the edge of your bed, waiting for you to wake up. You feel their presence and open your eyes. The night is a raven's wing, light doesn't penetrate it. They tell you stories about their bodies. They want to imprint them in your fingers, onto your tongue, so you speak their stories for them. In their hands they carry severed breasts, like small pots in which tumours have been planted.

I had three as well, says one of them, *like the scattered pellets of a little shotgun.*

On the ceiling a sun is now anchored. Its rays pour down the walls. Your tongue has swollen as though a river has flowed into your mouth. Their stories are the roots of trees, they branch out over you, meshing with your own story. You no longer know which is your truth. Some of those women hold their wombs in their open palms. You want to run away from them, to say *That's not my story*. They know your thoughts. *Wait a bit*, their eyes say. They're as black as olives, the way the Black Sea would be if it was actually black.

Some have empty hands and are buttoned up to the throat. You don't know whether they have boobs. You don't know what's hidden under their clothes, under their skin. They are the ones who travel through the wormholes of time.

We're your ancestresses, they say. *Your pain is inscribed in our cells, while you carry ours within you. Others will come too. To teach you.*

That is spoken by Medea. She is the first of the old ones to come. She doesn't want to talk about herself.

Time has worn my story out, betrayal is stronger than love, those are the only words I leave you with.

After her comes Medusa. Writhing snakes hiss above her stone head. She is miraculously beautiful. The snakes slide over your bed, tame and warm.

Look into my eyes. Never forget you are immortal. Look at this collection of statues, all those centuries I have resisted. You can die in a million ways, but it doesn't mean you won't stay alive. Those are her words of solace.

And you know already that Penthesilea will come. You don't even try to sleep, you lie awake, waiting for her. She comes in by herself. The other Amazons stay behind the mirror. There, on that side of the world, Boreas, the north wind, twines his fingers into their hair. They flutter like flags on a battlefield.

We're your sisters. Have you forgotten you're part of our tribe? A warrior woman. Lions roar in your heart. You too are the daughter of Ares, says Penthesilea.

On the walls, images of wars come to life. Here you are too, primordial. Your arms stretch, the arrow is primed, on its tip is a flaming torch. Your eyes gleam with an equal glow. Your feet fly over the defeated bodies. You are both bird and woman.

'Did we cut off our right breasts ourselves?' you ask. 'Is this all so I can stay true to myself, faithful to my origin?'

Sometimes we must renounce something to be what we are, is all she says.

In the mirror there's a commotion. The Amazons come into the room. They approach you in pairs, bend down and whisper their names and their pain into your ear.

Eat your fears like an apple, they all say unanimously as they leave.

You're ten. Certainly no more than that. You're piled into your stuffy old car. Dad smokes the whole way. You and your brother are sick in the back. You get to the seaside. At the beach you take off your dress. You're in just your bikini bottoms. You feel the inappropriateness of your nakedness as a cold, unexpected touch. You notice your nipples aren't flat spots on your chest any more but little raised bulges, two buds trying to bloom. You feel quite clearly that it isn't permissible to show your body like this.

There's a crowd. The beach is covered with colourful towels and reddening bodies. The sea murmurs. Tiny waves break on the shore. Children's voices are shrill and loud, they bounce off the sand and break on the waves. The sun beats down on you all relentlessly. It's hard to keep your eyes open.

You sit down on a towel. You've clasped your knees with your hands. You're hot. You don't dare take the few steps to the sea to hide in it. You don't know how long you sit like that. At times you feel you've never stirred from this place. You lower your head to your arms and look at your chest. Between your nipples, precisely in the middle, there's another small bulge. Red, and just as sensitive to the touch as the nipples. Fear is sharp and has cold breath. You think that your body resists the confines of normal transformation, that what's breaking out of you, appearing in these bumps, is so powerful it won't be satisfied with just two buds. You think your transformation will be more complete, more monstrous, more terrible. Completely outside the limits of what's real. The woman blossoming inside you (you know it's a woman who wants to get out, who wants to transform your body) won't be content with anything. Nothing's enough for her. You cry. You think you've become deformed forever. A monster with three boobs.

You think that for three days. You hide, you keep your T-shirt on. You don't go into the sea. You sit in the shade and say nothing, impervious and inconsolable. Then you gather your strength. You decide to show everyone. Bare your teeth in their faces. Show them you're stronger than anything, you, warrior on the verge of tears, which you resist. In the tent you put on just your bikini bottoms and set off for the beach. Mum stops you.

'What's this?' she asks.

You stop, your jaw tight, your fists clenched. Ready to be a monstrosity.

'Well, look at this,' she mumbles.

Then she comes up to you and pops the little pimple between your boobs.

Maybe it would be better if I walked. Kept walking until my thoughts slowed down. You're tired. You do nothing but sit. You've got a large glass of red wine in your hand (that occasional glass of wine is the only tranquillizer you'll take). And it's night. Windy and cold. Sharp-toothed February. You could get ill. Perhaps. You could even die.

Sometimes you think none of this is real. Really real. Or else that nothing exists outside your reality. You're stuck in the seedbed of the Matrix. Or else you're a metaphysical substitute for Truman from *The Truman Show*. You can die innumerable times. Each time you'll be born anew. Like the heroine of some nameless video game for which you've copied down all the cheat codes. Your life is eternal. You're eternal. You're here until you put everything together perfectly. You feel clearly all the places where you've died. Death comes easily, after every false step. Since autumn you've been on the same level. You keep repeating it. Each month, you must repeat each fall several times. Each death is a parting from a bit of you. A version of you. You die and are resurrected. You'll be imprisoned in that whirlpool until you play it faultlessly. You feel that quite clearly. Instead of fear, that realization brings solace.

The hardest thing is to speak about the children. To think about the children. You keep telling them you're not going to die. It's beginning to bother them. They're afraid of that excessive insistence. But they still believe you. Your son says, 'I'm glad you've got breast cancer, and not the real thing. No one dies of this.' You confirm that: 'Don't worry, I'm not going to die.' You look him in the eye. With your tired gaze you try to kill his fear. Your daughter is older. She knows far more. She is equally convinced. You don't manage to tell them anything other than that you'll survive. Sometimes their lips form questions. But no words come out of their throats. Perhaps they're afraid one of your replies will destroy their fragile belief in your immortality. The days stretch out, one after the other. It becomes increasingly difficult to speak. Articulating a question means acknowledging fear.

Then you discover Cathy. From *The Big C*. Cathy has melanoma, fourth stage. When she gets the diagnosis, she comes home, leaves her husband and becomes the opposite of what she was. Cathy goes through doctors and therapies. She tries to feel the life that's threatening to disappear. Every night, you lie in your bed and watch two or three episodes. Afterwards, you don't talk about yourself. You talk about her. Everything vague and unclear, terrifying and difficult about carcinoma you experience through Cathy. She is a magical object with whose help you are unravelling your destinies. Your virtual white magic voodoo doll. You watch the whole series till the last season, to the last three episodes. You abstain from them without a word. You're not prepared to let her die.

Your thoughts move slowly, stretched like a film in a cinema projection. They don't overtake one another. You hear them clearly. Words spoken to the end. In your head. In a monotonous voice. As though you were talking to someone who doesn't understand properly. *Maybe I need a new toothbrush*. That's a good sentence. You don't stop it with a ready answer. Right now all options have an equal chance. Nothing is taken as read. You've got violet varnish on your hands, you've got short nails. Those are your hands. You recognize them.

It's evening. Another day is behind you. Metal, grey, swollen with unspoken words. You're all eating pizza. You and the children. You're drinking wine. You laugh. You think how beautiful they are. *How beautiful they are!* You don't think about whether you'll be able to watch them grow up. That thought is forbidden. Unnecessary. Damaging. Your thoughts and words are submitted to controls. Good and acceptable. And the others. The others are immediately censored. You put them into quarantine, where they will be erased.

Later, you're getting ready for bed. You're in the bath-room. Brushing your teeth. You're leaning forward. In the mirror, you see the depression above your breasts. Above the prostheses that represent breasts. Your skin is dry and tired. Your eyes are dark, blue. Your pupils have devoured your irises. You don't feel anything. You just wonder if this is the way one dies.

Things you think about:

Maybe you'd like to have a cat. To sit on your lap and purr. And say nothing. While you cry. And it doesn't care. You don't have to think about how it feels. Yellowish-orange. Small. You'll call it Frida, after Frida Kahlo. Or Fyodor, if it's male, after Dostoevsky, of course. But what if it scratches the furniture? Does that matter? Should that matter now, when you're imagining it and you know you'll never get one because your children don't like cats?

You'd like to forget your fear. And then love. Without thought. With no tomorrow. One who loves you. It's so easy to love someone who doesn't love you. There's minimal risk. You're always on the losing end. Oh, how certain that is, so consoling.

Are you still here because there are important things ahead of you which you still have to do? Or do you just happen to be here? Just as you might not be?

Cannabis oil leaves a bitter taste in your throat. Like an inflammation. The intimation of a cough. So you drink lots of water. Water is good for chemotherapy. It cleans the system. It's important to drink a lot of water.

It's important to eat healthily. Vegetables. Fruit. Not red meat. Not chicken. Nor dairy products. Especially not sugar. Nor white flour. Nothing white. Just salads and seeds.

Beetroot isn't a vegetable. It's a split heart under your hand.

You can't stand people who tell you what you ought to eat and drink.

Nor those who look at you pityingly.

Especially those who say, 'You mustn't get tense when you have cancer.'

Perhaps you can't stand people altogether.

Things you don't want to think about:

Your children
Your boobs
Your cancer
Your bald head
Your death

You draw a line under the day. Tomorrow is Sunday. A Sunday when you're supposed to go to the mountains, to increase your leucocytes. A Sunday when you're supposed to help your son with his homework. A Sunday when you're supposed to have a good rest. A Sunday in which you're supposed to spend quality time with your children – talk to them, hear what they say, be smiley and cheerful.

Look at me, I'm happy, everything's fine, we're happy!

For the next week you won't be able to do anything. Not speak. Nor sit. Nor keep your eyes open. They'll shut themselves in their own rooms. Waiting for next Sunday, for you to surface. For you to start breathing slowly and deeply again. As though you were alive. As though you really were alive.

You're thirteen. You sleep in one room. Mum, Dad, your brother and you. You and your brother are in bunk beds. You're in the top one. The two of you and your mother go to bed at the same time. Dad hasn't come home yet. You feel warmth in your body. You know it's happiness. Happiness because of the closeness of the three of you. You close your eyes. You squeeze them tight. You imagine he's never going to come home again. You'll never hear his car coming into the courtyard again. You'd recognize it among thousands of different cars. You'll never again hear the outside door being opened by his hand. Before you see him, the speed of that sound tells you how much he's drunk. Now you're not thinking about any of that. You've closed your eyes. You persuade yourself that he won't come back. That he'll die. That thought is quite acceptable. It's not enough for him to go away, as then he could come back. He needs to die. Any kind of death. You don't go into details. They're not essential. You just want him not to come back. You imagine life without him. A life in which, you believe, happiness would be possible. You imagine all the things the three of you would do together. The places you'd go. Days filled with laughter. You feel warm and comfortable. You drift off to sleep. Then you hear the dull, tired, snarling sound of his car, and you cry.

A few days ago, Selma died. You didn't know her. Until she died, you weren't even sure her name really was Selma. Sanela? Sanja? Senka? Something beginning with 'S'. A woman whose name begins with 'S', who worked with Minja in the bank. For six months you've known that this woman exists, that she wakes up every morning and goes to work, this woman whose name begins with 'S' and whom you never see.

Healthy.

After having a breast removed, chemotherapy and radiation.

Healthy.

A survivor.

Now her hands have let go of the curtain that's been separating you from fear.

This morning you wake up afraid you've turned into Gregor Samsa. You don't dare open your eyes or move your body, frightened by the fluidity of your possible metamorphoses. You've been worn out by the days in which you won't let go. You hold on to yourself firmly. 'This is me and nothing will change me!' you yell. The nausea is too much. Your empty stomach protrudes bloated, bumpy, like over-leavened dough, while your fingers slide over your bald head. You're beginning to doubt. Your ego is falling apart, draining away into tiny insignificant fragments. They don't promise the possibility of returning to a whole, a meaningful whole that is you, saved from spilling over into different shapes.

You don't count the days. There are too many. *There's nothing to count*, you repeat to yourself. *I'm still me. These are my eyes. These are my eyes!* You won't give in. You hit out. You say *This isn't a battle, no battle is required, this is me.* You who are alive, you who are eternal. Stronger than anything. Than your body whose pain you won't acknowledge. The third chemotherapy session. The third day. There's nothing apart from nausea. You are the stomach that rises, up and down in an empty space, in the dark. In the silence where sounds penetrate sharp and painful from a distance. As though someone is crying. Sobbing. With a puffy face. You don't recognize that woman. That face under the bald head. Like a kaleidoscope, thousands of broken details now settle into an ugly image. *Remember your strength. Remember your strength* – that's your mantra.

Your mother sits in the living room. She makes sure the children don't come into the room while you're smoking a joint. So they don't see. So at least that doesn't need to be explained. Aida wasn't right, it doesn't make you feel better. The smoke increases the nausea. It adds an ugly taste to your mouth. Your mind, clouded and dislocated, becomes yet more agitated. Something wants to leap out of you. If the whole of you turned inside out, like a glove, you'd find it easier.

Outside, the spring is advancing persistently. Everything is twittering and singing. Buzzing. Too many sounds. Too much unconstrained life. You lower the blinds to match the world with your inner darkness. It doesn't help. You don't want to lie down, let yourself go. You can't, like last time, sit through it all in an armchair. In an armchair with your body draped over the arm. You refuse to be a patient. You walk, from one room to another. You feel something rising upwards in your stomach. You open your mouth. Nothing comes out. Not even your voice. You feel like running. You don't allow the balcony railing to contain you. You fly over it, like the three squares at once in the hopscotch game. You fly. The fall is quite inconsequential. The fall is comforting. After it comes peace. The calming finality of nothingness, freeing you from the spasms of pain.

It's windy. The balcony door swings. The glass reflects the minaret of a mosque, the crown of a nettle tree and blue sky.

I ought to go outside and walk, you think. Walk it all out of yourself. Leave the room tied tightly round your neck. You stay sitting, motionless.

Three days ago, in Oncology, you ran into Aida. She didn't have any hair any more either. Her face was tired and bloated. Her struggle more intense. Her movements more aggressive. You wondered whether you looked the same to her. You talked about your children. About her daughter, who is twenty and studying in America. She wanted to come home. Aida wouldn't let her. About your daughter and son. About all the things you didn't say to each other. You both waved your hands. You said that you were strong. That you'd get through it all. Quickly and easily. And then live, really live. Genuinely inhale everything lovely that's now slipping through your fingers. You drew an imaginary line that nothing bad could cross. Behind it were the two of you, untouchable. Your name was soon called. You went to the day clinic. You forgot about Aida. Sometime later you'd remember you didn't ask her what her surname is now. You won't know how to find her to keep your agreement: a morning coffee, a meeting of bald heads at the Bristol Hotel. 'Look at us, nothing hurts, there's nothing wrong, we can do anything,' you both sobbed.

In this third session as well, you resisted for six days. Your blackened eyes that had devoured your pupils, your gaze transformed into the gaze of death, stand like a wall opposite you in the mirror. Your breath is slow, difficult, and you ask *Have you come for me?* Maybe you're even ready for it to be over. Not through the illness. You won't agree to that. But there are moments when you'd like to end it in your own way.

You keep going until the seventh night. The seventh night is sleepless. A night of an onrush of energy. You don't close your eyes. The world falls apart then restores itself to perfect sense. At last you're returning to yourself. A night of rapid thoughts and perfect calm. The following day is a little easier for you. You even breathe a bit. Some food can already slip down your throat. You go to the bathroom. You look for it in the mirror. You tell it *Come on! Show yourself! Hit me with all you have! I'm stronger than you!*

Death, present now only as a blue shadow under your eyes, is silent.

From mirrors, switched-off television sets and glass-framed pictures on the wall, your bald head sneaks up on you. An instant in which you have to remember that this is you. And why it's you. Last night you woke up writing a letter to your father, who died nearly sixteen years ago. He was standing beside you, hazy and faint, out of focus, a silhouette losing its edge. He asked you why you didn't write more fiercely, more angrily. Why you didn't tell all those people where to stick it. He certainly would have. You thought he couldn't hear you, and that's why you began to write. Or you began to write because it's only when you write that you really think. Or because it's only then you know you exist. You wrote black letters on white paper torn out of a small, lined exercise book: *When I write, others really don't exist. At best, they are functions. I write only to seize the moment. And myself in it.*

You woke up with hiccups. For the third time that night. You stopped thinking both about writing and your father. And whether you'd have talked about those things with him at all if he was alive. You got up for a third time. You got a sugar cube. You dunked it briefly in water, put it in your mouth and waited for it to dissolve. You thought about the fact that you've heard a million times in the last six months that you mustn't eat sugar. Or dairy products. Or red meat. Or chicken. It seemed more important to you to think about why you had hiccups, for a third time. Because of yesterday's chemotherapy, or anxiety? And your throat hurt. It was tightness rather than pain. Was that from nerves? You decided it was all because of nerves and went back to bed. You couldn't sleep.

In the morning, you go to see your GP. Your throat really is red. You're annoyed that you never take yourself seriously enough. You always think there's nothing wrong with you. Even the cancer. You think that it too isn't real. Only nerves are real. The psyche which imagines everything. That child in you, the one you were long ago, is still asking for attention. As though aware of what you're thinking, she says: *But hiccups can be caused by nerves.* You need those nerves, to convince yourself you're still capable of feeling. That you haven't reached the point when you know everything is futile and life is nothing other than pain, occasionally shaken by tremors of love.

You go home and light a joint. To calm yourself and reduce the nausea. You don't know whether that's why you light up or whether it's because you miss smoking. A cigarette with your morning coffee, which you have at noon, after you've tidied the house, been to the shop, or even cooked lunch. The children are at school. A big cup of coffee, computer and a cigarette. You breathe. You're alive. You don't feel that when you light a joint. A pang of conscience spoils it. Maybe it's been lit for the wrong reason. You don't drink coffee any more either. You've never been a great one for coffee. You only made it because of the size of the cup, to prolong the ritual, the time for breathing, the time for existing.

Now, you start the day with a fresh vegetable and fruit juice, into which anything goes, from mango to kale. A little later you have a slice of brown bread. You don't know what to eat it with, now you can't eat dairy or dried meat products. For lunch you make soups of lentils and vegetables, wholegrain rice, vegetables in a million ways, particularly raw, and a big green salad with carrots, beetroot and roast flax, pumpkin, sunflower and sesame seeds. After lunch you drink an immunity powder that tastes like water in which a rotten chestnut has been soaked. In the afternoon you eat popcorn, for your leucocytes. During the day, you're also supposed to stuff yourself with hazelnuts, almonds, pieces of apricot stones, vitamin C, propolis and a whole lot of other things you mostly forget to take. For supper you've had enough of everything and order pizza. You spread it with mayonnaise, put the box on your lap, your feet on the table and watch TV. You pour yourself a glass of wine as well and think: *Fuck cancer, fuck you all!* Paraffin from Albania, special honey made by special people in a cave in Montenegro, all kinds of herbs that cure everything, germanium, graviola and all kinds of other nonsense millions of well-intentioned people shower you with every day. You reject their unconscious mission to throw you into a state of panic, driving you into a merciless race for a magic potion that will save you. You eat your pizza. Mayonnaise mixed with thick tomato sauce runs down your chin. You're happy. The television screen goes blank for a moment, and you catch sight of your bald head again.

Fuck you! you tell it.

As long as you can remember, you've spent the summers on the Pelješac peninsula. In a small village, hidden in a magical bay, with stone houses facing the translucent sea. That place is your true home. That sandy shore and tireless blue. It's only there that what's within you and what's outside equalize, create a symmetry that enables you to breathe. Salt in the air leaves a sweetish taste in your mouth. That place is either the beginning or the end of the world. There's no need to escape from it. On one of the slopes that surround the village and dive into the sea there's a tree. You don't know what sort. You've never seen it close up. It's too far away for you to get near it. It grows differently from any other tree you've ever seen – leaning against the hill at a right angle. A long thin trunk and a big many-branched crown. It refuses to grow like other trees. It's your tree. Every summer, when you arrive, you run to check it's still there.

You're enchanted by the sea. By the power of the water, its waves and its blueness. By the solace with which it tries to wash the world. Sometimes you dream you're a fish. You'll enter the sea. Immerse yourself in that freedom. Never come back. Mostly you stand in the water up to your hips and drink in the peace. You imagine you're about to start swimming and go far away, to the island of Mljet or Korčula. The only thing stronger than your obsession with the sea is your fear of it. You open your eyes under the water. Everything is dark, the vague outlines of the dancing light look like sharks. Enraged sharks that want to sink their teeth into your flesh. And your body streaks back to the shore the same instant.

Once you dream you are swimming with your brother. You have gone some distance from the shore. The sea is warm. The sky is blue. First you hear a sound. The sea is choppy. Then you catch sight of them. A whole shoal of sharks. Enormous silver bodies with huge wide-open jaws. They circle round you. Their fins cut through the water. They aim for your brother. They bite off pieces of his body. They mutilate him. The sea is a frothing red blot. A boiling soup. You hit out to save him. You feel their slippery skin under the water. They slide over you. They don't want you. They want him. You can't help him, however much you hit out, however much you scream. You wake up crying. The water moves away from you. The redness disappears. All that's left is the fading darkness of a summer dawn, dappled with the voices of cicadas.

People's glances quickly pass over you. The way they wince gives them away. A wince that says: *I'm not looking at you, you're the same as everyone else, imagine that I think you're the same as everyone else, that's why I'm not looking at you*. You're still carrying your bald head around like a flag. It's your choice. Your freedom. If you cover it up, someone might think you're afraid. In the darkness of the cinema you let your tears fall, only because you're sure your mascara really is waterproof. You've leaned your head on your son's and you smell him. He doesn't know you're crying. On the screen a man is killing another man. Without any reason that would justify his action. Because of some phantom he has long carried in himself. A phantom that has nothing to do with the man now lying in the snow, in a pool of blood. A bullet fired just like that. And death comes just like that. Your bodies jerk at the sound of the shot. Although you saw the pistol. You jerk as much at the second and third shots. You allow the silence to enter you slowly. A silence that will last long after you leave the cinema. A silence louder than the words with which you try to break it in the car, on the way home. Louder than the television you put on even before you take off your coats. Heavier than the duvet you cover yourselves with when you get into bed, thinking you'll feel better if you're together as you tremble at the bullet aimed at you. Just like that.

TAXOL

Special indications: Paclitaxel (Taxol) should be administered under the supervision of a doctor with experience in the use of chemotherapeutic agents in the treatment of tumours. In view of the fact that significant reactions may appear in patients experiencing severe hypersensitivity, appropriate equipment for supportive treatment must be accessible. Because of possible extravasation, careful monitoring of the infusion site throughout the administration of the drug is advised. Before receiving paclitaxel, patients must receive premedication consisting of corticosteroids, histamine antagonists of H1 receptors (antihistamine) and histamine antagonists of H2 receptors. When used in combinations, paclitaxel must be administered before cisplatin.

You think the worst is over. Taxol is nothing compared to AC therapies. Taxol is twelve weeks, twelve doses which are borne more easily. They'll make the only hairs on your body, your eyebrows and eyelashes, fall out. And maybe your nails. Or the nails may just turn black. You're prepared for that. Just as long as they've finished with the AC. AC is Adriamycin cyclophosphamide, the reason you hate the colour red. You've bought four bottles of black nail polish. You read on the internet that painting your nails with black polish helps to retain them, or at least to disguise the way they really look. You're ready.

You lie on the bed, waiting. There are three chairs beside you. On one of them is Vera. You've been seeing her for a long time now, every time you come. In the waiting room, in the corridors, in this room where you're both hooked to tubes through which pour poisons meant to cure you. Vera talks. Without drawing breath. In a squeaky voice with no modulation. From her mouth a river flows, ceaselessly narrating an illness, the history of her illness, the illnesses of those she has been meeting in these gloomy rooms for three years now, since she began her treatment. You avoid her eyes. You don't want to hear her. You don't want to answer her questions, after which, like a ping-pong ball, the story will return to what happened to her. Up to now you've managed to avoid her each time. You know she's talking to you, two chairs away to the left, although it seems she is talking to the woman beside her. You look straight ahead, you try not to hear her. You wait for the needle to finally penetrate your vein. You're pretending that this time, when you start the Taxol, the three nurses are there by your bed by chance, and not in case of allergic reactions. But then you hear her, this time determined to reach you.

'It doesn't suit anyone as well as it does her and Donna Ares.'

She means your bald head. It's rare to be uncovered in Oncology. You can't help laughing. You turn and look at her. For the first time you really see her eyes, washed out with fear. You talk. It only lasts a few minutes, because you're already asleep. The Taxol is doing its thing. Taxol is a temporary blackout. Instant transition into sleep. Sleep without thoughts, without dreams. Sleep that doesn't rest you. Sleep like a brief fall into nothingness out of which you return as you were to everything that remained behind you. A pointless intermezzo that destroys the dimension of time.

Before you fell asleep you replied to Vera's question about whether you were HER2-positive. She is as well. And, like her, you'll be getting Herceptin. Herceptin is a miraculous medicine for those of you who have the most aggressive, hysterical type of cancer. Your cells are filled with the HER2 protein. It sends them into overdrive, into uncontrolled mass production, ceaseless work in three shifts, without a moment's pause. Until some seven years ago Herceptin wasn't included in clinical treatment, so you and Vera didn't have the chance of avoiding it. Vera has been on it for two and a half years already. You'll take it for a year. Seventeen doses, one every three weeks.

'Herceptin's nothing. Nothing. As though you haven't taken anything. Here, look at me. Nothing. For two and a half years already. Yes. Yes. Every three weeks. What can you do? But no matter. You go home the way you came. You'll see. No problems. None at all. Only one woman here has ever died when they gave her the first dose. But otherwise, nothing. Nothing …'

You endure the Taxol well. There's no nausea. And you don't die. But in the evening tiny hard spots start appearing on your stomach, legs and neck. You end up in A & E. Your body refuses it. The following days are spent visiting doctors who have to decide what to do next. Each of them has a different opinion. Keep going with Taxol. Stop the Taxol. Do tests for which there are no facilities in this town. Try again and see what happens. You're not prepared for that. You don't want the next allergic reaction. The anticipation of how bad it might be. You say you don't want any more. You don't accept new dimensions of fear for the next eleven weeks. They put you back on AC. You'll have to have two more treatments. The red fluid will be poured into your body twice more. Flow through your tired veins. Fly through you, making your first urine just as red, unnaturally red, like diluted pinkish blood. Two more periods of nausea which dull the consciousness and make the world a dubious place which you can't be certain is truly real.

Now, as you wait for the Taxol to be cleared from your organism so you're ready for the next round of AC, you've been given an unplanned ten-day pause. An unexpected spring holiday to sit on the balcony and feel the life pulsating in you. That's when you make all your decisions. How you'll do things differently. Make the moments conscious, not let them escape from you. Feel your breath filling your lungs and then leaving you. Your children's laughter splashes your body like a waterfall. That will be enough. Quite enough.

Then you'll put on your wig for the first and last time. For a friend's wedding. You'll wear a nice black dress and black high-heeled shoes. Your wig is white, unnaturally white, metallic white. A pageboy cut, with a fringe. You'll take it off after just an hour. You'll tell everyone it was rubbing. You lie. You can't bear the concealment. You dance. Your body is fluid. The music glides over you. It seeps into your cells. The world is laughter. You don't stop till dawn. In the end all that remains on the dance floor will be your body. Liberated.

Hospitals are a space you've always known. From your twelfth to your twenty-sixth year your father will be dying. Dedicatedly and systematically. He'll end up in hospital every six months. And each time he'll be brought back from that cliff, dragged back, into the life in which his body refuses to participate.

You're fifteen. You're waiting for an ambulance. You sit beside him. His body is cold and sweaty. Completely white. His eyes seek yours, for you to acknowledge, although he isn't sure what he's done wrong, that you understand he didn't know any better. The proximity of death, the possibility of his final departure, means you're ready to forgive him everything.

The room is filled with a strange, strong, sweet smell. It's like the smell of jasmine. At first you think it's coming in through the window. Then you realize it's coming from him, from his body. You know it's the smell of death. You're afraid it will take you too. You want to get up. To run away from the room. But you stay sitting there, you take hold of his hand, hold it tightly, so he feels you, so he knows he's not alone. Perhaps you try to tear him away from that smell. Perhaps that's precisely when your open, frantic, bloody battle with death begins. You hold his hand, look into his eyes and smile. Maybe you say something, you don't remember. It's hard to imagine the words you both say then or at any other moment. You know only that he doesn't take his fixed, wide-open gaze from you. You are the buoy he has caught hold of, while the two of you suffocate in that sweet, increasingly strong, increasingly intoxicating smell.

Later, the ambulance takes him away. You go to the bathroom, you scour your body under hot water. You open your mouth wide and let the water pour into you. That smell has penetrated each of your cells. You strain to vomit, to purge it. Sometimes you think you've not succeeded, that the trace of him has stayed in you forever, a little rotten spot from where the decay of your body begins.

Afterwards, you can't eat for days. You can't bear any kind of smell any more. Once again, you're that little girl in whom something is crying. You can't even allow food into your mouth. Your body is changing. Every day it's thinner, more fragile, more brittle. *A sorry sight* indeed.

It's the fourth day of your fifth chemotherapy treatment. Until yesterday it's gone reasonably well. Until the afternoon you think that this time you are stronger. That it won't break you. Then you begin to slip slowly into an abyss. Into something black and sticky that muddles your thoughts until they're unrecognizable and doesn't let you breathe. You can't get hold of anything. Resistance may only slow that free fall. You're under the shower. You've wrapped your arms around yourself. You let the water beat the nape of your neck. You watch the droplets overtaking each other. They slide over your forearm, making an uninterrupted river to the floor. The touch of the water soothes you. Something in that flowing convinces you life cannot stop.

You feel the little lump, the stone under your skin, the seed out of which the future that's now stifling you developed on that hot night two days after you returned from Montenegro, from two days sailing in a small yacht. Four of you, old friends, on an endeavour to experience the world without gravity. The four of you and the sea stretching out around you. Cheese, olives and wine. A sea calm and dark. The boat cuts through it. You carve out a furrow from which it quickly recovers. You don't leave any real trace as you sail over it. Just a moment, and then it's as though you haven't been there.

There's no oblivion so absolute. The blue parts in front of you. Enabling your journey. Swallowing the memory of you.

You anchor in the middle of the Bay of Kotor, as if in an open shell. You're drunk. You jump into the water. For the first time with no fear. Your body breaks the surface. It sinks deep into the black warmth. The sea embraces you. Wraps around every fragment of your body. It rocks you slowly. There's nothing more tender than water. It's warm and dense, lulled into its own darkness. It accepts you like a perfectly fitting glove. It caresses you as it tries to wash away anything that might hurt. You think that if God exists He surely sleeps in the depths of the Bay of Kotor. You think you ought to be a fish. Your body is expiring without water. Wilting without salt. You're ready to stay here forever.

Now, under the shower, you close your eyes. You feel scales emerging from your skin. Your body is supple and slippery. It will easily slip out of the hands of death.

You're seventeen. Your father's had a heart attack and has a twisted gut. Perhaps just one of the two. The doctors aren't certain. They send him from one hospital to another. They try to work out from which place his body is now abdicating. You're all exhausted by his illnesses already. Word gets round the town that he's died. A neighbour comes into your house in tears. She finds you polishing the dining room table, pressing into it as though you're sanding it. You sense something, maybe you've already half-heard something. You don't remember any more. You run your hands swiftly over the brown wooden board. That's all that concerns you. Its steady shine. You're out of breath. You're sweating. You don't stop.

'My condolences, my dear.'

She holds out her hand. You put down the rag. You hold out your own hand. That's what you do at a time like that. When someone holds out their hand you do the same. Words have no meaning. You're focused on movements. When she touches you, you feel sick. You take back your hand, but she doesn't give up. She wants to hug you. To start with, you push her gently away. She doesn't let go. You start to hit her. With your fists, with all your strength. Alarmed by the screams, Mum comes in from the next room. She tries to wrest your crazed body away from the poor woman. They're saying something. You can't hear them. You push them both away. You go somewhere. You don't remember where. Maybe you're in your room. Maybe you're not. You're not aware of space. Or of time. Something heavy is sticking to you and hurting. Later, someone comes and tells you he's alive. You try to be glad. You don't feel anything.

You see him a week later. There are ten beds in the room. You walk past his. You glance at him. You don't recognize him. Morphine can do that, they say, transform you, suck everything out of a person. You sit beside his feet. He looks at you with empty eyes. He tries to smile. The silence between you is a spider's web from which words can't be disentangled.

You're trying to remember yourself as a child. The image escapes you. It's the third day of the sixth dose. You resist the gravity that wants to pin you to the bed. Your thoughts are scattered, weary. They can't form a firm sentence. You need that old you, that little girl. You know you must tell her something, something comforting, after which a different kind of life will follow. Take you away from the place you are now. You're quite certain: time is a gut twisted into a knot. You let your voice flow through it. To reach her. You don't succeed in summoning her. Because of the nausea, it's easier when you keep your eyes closed. You're not afraid of that darkness. It's yours. You know yourself too well inside by now. The silence with which the darkness speaks is final. Maybe that's the comfort you want to offer her. Your thought isn't capable of catching its beginning or end. You're sure of nothing apart from the fact that everything slips away. Now you think time is a broken harmonica. It keeps you apart, there's not a single note where you can meet.

Your hair is growing, sharp as wire. Every few days you shave your head. Your scalp prickles when you lie down. Now it's different, softer. Maybe it will stay. Having hair is the first step back to yourself. Your daughter comes in. She hugs you. Her embrace is a little respite. A brief moment in which everything stops hurting.

'Why's your head so grey?' asks your son.

In the bathroom, you see that your hair is growing back completely grey. Grey hair above a greying face. You rummage through the drawers looking for hair dye. You find a tube of blonde. You mix it. You dye your hair. You can't keep your eyes open. Your stomach is in your throat. Each inhalation is a disc on a weighing scale, and the wrong distribution can start you vomiting. You think it might never stop. And with all the poison inside you, it's not good to add to it. But you feel a calm. You've created a space to make decisions about yourself. Somewhere in front of you an end can be glimpsed.

You're back in the armchair. You'll be here for the next three days, stronger than before. Again, you're convinced the worst is over. You know that somewhere, in the blackest darkness inside you, there's calm. The spark from which you came. There you can come back to life a million times. There, not one death can kill you. Reality has been rearranged in a thousand layers. Snares that block you on the path to yourself, to the place where your salvation lies. It's close, as though you've dreamed that path, as though you've seen it before. It looks like the way to school when you were a child and it was snowing. Up a slope. It's icy. You slip. You're little, it's hard, you don't know if you'll make it. But you feel clearly that the obstacle on the path is just a mistake in reality. A stitch in a dress that's gone wrong. You know you must hold on to the wall with both hands, close your eyes firmly and reach the place where you reset the world.

You're very small. You're all living in Gran and Grandad's house. You sleep in a room with them. Grandad lulls you to sleep every night. You sleep on a three-seater settee that turns into a large bed. You're in the middle. You go to bed long before them. Grandad goes with you. He sits beside you until you fall asleep. Maybe longer. You don't know. You sink into sleep convinced he'll always be there. The bed is big. Your body is small. He holds your foot. You ask him to do that. 'Grandad, hold my foot.' Up to now there has never been a more comforting touch. His hand is warm. It fits into the curve of your sole. Fills that arc. Presses emptiness away. There's no part of you that's not protected. Sometimes you think that everything that comes later is just an attempt to feel that touch.

Before New Year, you all decorate a large plastic fir tree on a little table beside the sofa. Mum climbs onto a chair and takes down the boxes containing the tree and the ornaments. Each ornament is different. They're fragile. So delicate you don't dare breathe when she hands them to you. You arrange them by the tree. She carefully takes them out of their newspaper wrappings, takes them by the thread attached and hands them to you. You're horribly afraid you'll break them. That will make Mum sad. Your mum's sadness is a thick duvet whose end you can't see. Afterwards, you place little lights on the tree. You put cotton wool on the sharp plastic branches like snow. Finally, Mum lifts you up to put the big gold star on the top.

Later, you go to bed. The little lights are on. They go on and off. Light of different colours dances through the room. Grandad is holding your foot.

HERCEPTIN

A small bottle contains 150 mg of trastuzumab, a humanized IgG1 monoclonal antibody produced in a culture of CHO cells in suspension (CHO cells are cells from the ovaries of the Chinese hamster) and purified using affinity and ion-exchange chromatography including the specific deactivation of the virus and steps to remove it.

Trastuzumab is a humanized IgG1 monoclonal antibody that interferes with the HER2 receptor. Herceptin is a sterile, white to pale yellow powder for intravenous administration. Its main role is the treatment of certain kinds of breast cancer. HER2 receptors are proteins built into the cell membrane so are tasked with carrying molecular signals from the surroundings of the cell to its interior. Each HER2 receptor is made up of an external and internal cell domain. The external domain may bind ligands, while the internal domain activates protein kinases signalling pathways. HER2 proteins (receptors) initiate cell proliferation, growth and survival. In some types of cancer, particularly certain types of breast cancer, HER2 is overexpressed and so causes the uncontrolled division of cancer cells.

Studies of trastuzumab show that it extends overall survival in the later (metastatic) stage of breast cancer from 20.3 to 25.1 months. In the early stage of breast cancer, it reduces the risk of the return of the cancer after an operation by 9.5%, and the risk of death by 3%. It may increase the risk of cardiac disease by 2.1%, which can be solved by stopping the treatment. Trastuzumab is also being studied for the treatment of other kinds of cancer that express the HER2 receptor.

It's May. Outside, the world is chirping and buzzing. Intoxicated. From your balcony you can see Vahida's garden. Taib, her son, died sometime last winter. Or autumn. You no longer remember. Time has no meaning. Its passing is measured in therapies, not minutes. His cancer was on his lungs. That's all you know. This year not a single rose grew in Vahida's garden.

Taib is one of the forbidden thoughts. And Vahida's roses are a forbidden thought because they lead to Taib. You're not sure what you feel when you think about such things. You and the world, connected by the law of communicating vessels, are reaching a point where even fear doesn't exist. Just a weary, sated sorrow.

You told yourself: *The worst is over. It's all past already. You won't even feel what's to come.*

But Herceptin comes. Seventeen doses. Every three weeks an injection in the thigh. The drug burns in your flesh. They inject it slowly, drop by drop. A large red circle appears around the prick. As the day goes by, it pales gradually, under cold compresses. It's transformed into a large, swollen, white mark. You're glad. Only a month ago, Herceptin was given only into a vein. Your veins wouldn't have tolerated another seventeen pricks, along with the seventeen blood samples that prove you're capable, ready to take that blow. You keep repeating: *How glad I am! How glad I am!*

You're also taking Tamoxifen. The carcinoma was hormone-positive. Tamoxifen is meant to stop the production of oestrogen and progesterone. Two tablets a day, for the next ten years. 'That's just fine,' you say. You don't read the instructions in the leaflet that list all that can go wrong. You say your body is ready. That it wants this. That it needs help. That it agrees.

Before you stretches the summer. And health. Life. The happiness for which you've waited so long. From this point on only good can come. You're quite certain of that.

From the outset your periods are painful. Over time they become heavier. They come in the night. You can feel that rearrangement in yourself for days in advance, the fear that it's opening up all the cracks through which pain can creep in. All the holes that you mend for the rest of the month. You sew them up. You convince yourself they're not there.

You're woken by pain. Below your stomach and in your pelvis. It seems that your vagina is so open that the whole of you is going to seep out of it. Only small, rare, dark drops emerge from you. You spend the first hour in the bathroom. On the toilet. That's easiest for you. You hold a basin on your lap. You feel nauseous, you think you're going to be sick. Throw yourself out of your mouth. You've poured brandy into a glass. You sip it slowly. Otherwise you don't drink, you're too young. They told you it hurts because the blood can't start flowing. You need to warm your body with alcohol first. You don't know whether it helps.

After an hour or so, after a few attempts, you'll manage to make it to the living room. You'll wrap your pelvis and stomach in a big woollen shawl. Even in summer. Sit in an armchair. There's one cushion behind you, and you press into it. The other's underneath you. Your legs are raised. You're doubled up. You wait for it to pass. Your thoughts are scattered. You'd like to be small. To have your Grandad beside you. Holding your foot. The tree is decorated. The colours run into each other as you sink into sleep.

There's no one around. It's night and everyone's asleep.

You sit there for hours. Every time. Waiting. Your body is dividing somewhere deep inside. It wants to break in half. To separate enough for the blood to run, to reduce the pain. You wait for dawn and go to your bed, drained. Once again you've survived the process of becoming a woman.

The moment when consciousness is extinguished is the final transition into nothingness. You don't know that yet. You tell yourself that it's weakness you're feeling, constant fatigue, the consequence of Herceptin. That it's normal.

It will start with the menstrual period that comes seven months after Taxol interrupted that process.

It's the beginning of September, early morning. You're woken by chirruping birds under the window and by pain. You separate yourself from sleep with difficulty. You try to remember where you are. You think you're in water, in warm water. The sea in the Bay of Kotor has boiled over. Thickened. You can't move your legs. You're sinking. You can't breathe. As though someone's holding your head down. Pushing you down. You jerk your body. You wake with a cry. You open your eyes wide and sit up in bed. A big, dark blot of blood is spreading round you.

The following evening, you end up in hospital. The flow can't be stopped. It runs down your legs as you walk. In the hospital they give you an injection. They stop the bleeding. You feel relieved. You're convinced you've dodged yet another bullet. Maybe you have even died one of your unconscious deaths. You don't know. But the fatigue doesn't let up. You want only to lie down. You want someone to love you so much that their love brings you completely back to life. You clutch your lover's hand like a straw.

You've acquired a cat. Small. Orange. You call her Frida. She's supposed to ensure that life goes on. With her warmth, her body that exudes calm, she's supposed to warm all the empty spaces in your house where dread has settled.

A few days later, you discover that you have a temperature. Not high. Only 37.3. But nothing will bring it down. Your fatigue is unceasing. You start visiting doctors. You get up in the morning, you go to one of them. You notice that your right breast is slightly swollen. You have to go for another MRI. To make sure it hasn't come back. That a new one hasn't appeared. Sneaked in at a moment of inattention.

That morning when you go for the scan, you get your period again. Nothing can stop the blood that doesn't want to stay inside you. You're in a hospital gown. You're sitting on the edge of a bed. Nurses come one after another, trying to inject a cannula into your hardened vein. Then they put a nappy on you. So they don't make the scanner bloody. They don't know what to do with you and all that blood. They haven't been trained to work with people like you. It's a private clinic. You drove yourselves here this morning, to Sarajevo, you and your mother, because the scanner in your town is broken. You lie in the iron jaws that shake, in an impossible position, on your stomach, with your arms stretched forwards, your legs raised, swallowed, on the edge of consciousness, unprepared for all the bad that wants to reach you.

The results are good. There's no new carcinoma. A prosthesis has not burst. Everything looks quite in order. But your boob keeps growing. Your temperature won't go down. And you're increasingly tired. Broken. You feel the fragments that bind themselves into your body, now almost ready to give up. You want only to sleep, to hide, to run away for a moment from a fear that for the first time you are unable to escape.

After the scan, you drive back home. You try to think of your lover. He and the real life beyond the hospital walls, everything outside the heaps of paper on which are written the words and numbers that seek to tie the story of your body into a meaningful whole, pass you by. You're convinced you'll never find the way back.

Instead of home, you go to the hospital. You're too weak. The flow is a wild river. A torrent demolishing everything in front of it. They stop you menstruating again. This is too risky. They say: 'The womb and ovaries have to be removed.' You don't hear the reasons. You don't hear anything. You wonder whether you'll be a woman after that. Without breasts, a womb, ovaries. A woman without the body of a woman. You're almost indifferent. It's just one more thing you must do, just another part of you that you have to give up in order to remain.

They must do the operation as soon as possible. Before your next menstrual period. Your blood test is bad. They don't know whether you can survive this intervention. They don't know why the blood won't stay inside you. The power of that revolt confuses them. Your temperature won't go down. Your breast is growing. Now it's a bit red. Your anaemia worsens, making the operation impossible. You drink a load of supplements to improve your blood. It refuses, it's had enough.

You don't know how long this lasts. Four or five weeks. There isn't a single organ in your body that hasn't been examined. Every examination is a new alarm. Something is resisting in every part of your body. Every day another death is scheduled. You reject it. You won't comply. You're unable to stay in the channel you've been digging for a year now and you won't let fear creep in. Now, nothing exists apart from that fear. That's because of the anaemia. Your brain is not getting enough oxygen. It feels as though someone is suffocating you. That's why your body mutinies. It keeps trying to take that invisible hand from its mouth and nose. Your brain is hysterical, crazed by your frenzied tremor. Your hand in your lover's is the only thread that binds you to reality.

You go to the hospital every morning. They carry out various tests. The rest of the day you wait. Your blood won't improve. They look for internal bleeding, a crack, a hole through which the blood is escaping, causing your system to collapse. Each new day, a new examination is a diversion to nothing, to yet another question the answer to which eludes them.

You're huddled up on the sofa. You no longer resist lying down. Your thoughts are rapid, panic-stricken, as though your two eyes see two different images. For the first time you think that this is perhaps the end.

You're twelve. You don't remember whether you have been in a hospital before your father's first heart attack. You don't remember how long he's been lying in that four-bed room, with shabby bed linen, when your mother takes you both to see him. All you remember is the cold of the corridor, although it's summer and hot outside. You're afraid of this space. You forget to breathe. Your chest feels tight. He's lying in bed wearing blue pyjamas with buttons. You've never seen him in pyjamas before. He always sleeps naked, in just his underpants. His face is sunken and pale. He doesn't look like himself. You almost don't recognize him. Mum takes the food out of a bag she's brought. She tidies the bedside table. She puts the dirty things into the bag to take home. She's busy. You and your brother stand and say nothing.

'What's happening at school?' he asks you.

'Nothing,' you say.

You look at his face. You try to say something else. You can't think of anything, so you start looking at the floor.

'How about you, mate?' he says to my brother.

'Nothing,' he replies.

You're both silent again. All that can be heard is the rustling of the plastic bag under your mother's fingers.

Afterwards, on your way out, through the same cold corridors, Mum and your brother hurry ahead of you. You follow them, gazing at the photographs on the walls. You're not looking where you're going. A large concrete post halts your steps. You collide with it hard. Head first. The sound inside you is dull and echoing. Your knees feel weak and you fall to the floor. For the rest of the day your head rings, the sound spreads through you. As though you've swallowed it and now it can't find a way out of you.

Its echo rings in you to this day, every time you cross the hospital threshold.

Now the women no longer visit you at night. The moon's glow is a milky mark on the wall. The ceiling doesn't let worlds capable of consoling you through. You know it's time for you to go on a journey.

The sky is a metal plate. It reproduces the silence, the smudged colours of your unease. You go south. That's where you must find them. The stiff helichrysum is an intimation of winter. Black and green eyes watch you from the olive trees. Pines embrace each other with their roots and entwine their arms in a prayer for the wholeness of your body. The mountain slopes fall headlong into the sea. The coast has sprinkled the open sea with islands. Salt murmurs in the air. Waves forge secret paths. In the depths, plankton glistens. The fish are silver. Their clockwork mechanisms count down eternity.

You find Medea in a cave. She's turned her back to the light. She doesn't recognize you. Her tears are a salt river, a waterfall that roars and rebounds off the rocks.

It would be better for you to move on, you won't find anything here. And what could you ask from a woman like me? Haven't they listed my misdeeds a hundred times? Wild woman. Crazed with love for poor Jason, that's what they say. Who's still interested in my truth? Go. I can't help you.

You slide over the surface of the sea, as over a frozen lake, to a rocky island with a garden of male bodies made of stone. The snakes in Medusa's hair have fallen asleep.

This isn't a dream. Death is a passing illness. Run, she says. *For a woman, every battle is already lost.*

She lowers her eyes. Her death can't bring you back to life.

A little further on, at a place where the sea opens to receive a river, the delta hides the bodies of dead Amazons. Their hair is river weed, swayed by the water.

'Penthesilea! Penthesilea!' you call.

I was slain by the hand of Achilles. Now I'm just one of the corpses strewn over the pages of history. Defeated. Her eyes are shells, filled with mud.

'We are the Moon's warriors, daughters of Ares!' you shriek.

Your voice reverberates off their bodies. They've already turned to glass. The scars on their chests stare into your eyes.

Water remembers. Only water will carry the outlines of our pain into eternity.

That's the last thing you hear. You're swallowed by mist. It's hot and fierce, as though it's bubbling out of the hatch to the world under your bed. The bed is deep and narrow, like a grave from which you will never rise.

September has melted into October. On the fifteenth, you stay in hospital. The operation is scheduled for the seventeenth. They hope they'll be able to operate. Until the fifteenth they've been doing tests every day. They pass different machines over your body. They take samples of blood, urine, stool. On each of the three preceding mornings, including that Monday when the air becomes sharp, announcing an autumn indifferent to your dread, you go to the intensive care unit at seven o'clock. There, struggling with your veins, they take blood. They send it for analysis, in the search for a strange bacterium that's settled in your bloodstream and is destroying you internally, from your blackest depths. On the third morning, after taking blood, the most skilled medical teams alternate over your arm. They look for a vein that will take a cannula. After an hour of unsuccessful attempts, while your hands and theirs shake, they succeed in inserting a small, child's one. Your arm refuses, this time truly, definitively and stubbornly refuses. Your trembling, tormented, exhausted body no longer trusts anyone and rejects everything.

Some hours earlier, you're standing in the corridor of the intensive care unit. There are two doors in front of you. You wait. A cleaner opens one, swabs the floor in front of it and leaves it open. It's a room with about ten beds. She's lying on the first one. At first you don't recognize her. Her pale, pale body. Bald head. By now, she should have had hair. Aida. You look at each other. For a long time there are no words. They are stuck in your throats like fish bones. She's naked, under a large sheet that covers her up to her chest. You're a few metres from her. She stretches out her arms. You think *How long and lovely her arms are*. You think she looks like a bird. Her arms are open as though they are surrendering, finally surrendering, ripping the air. Her lips say only one thing: *horror, horror, horror, horror*. That word is a tremor that will not emerge from her mouth. Now you know what that place after which there is nothing looks like. Her eyes too repeat: *horror, horror, horror*. Only afterwards will you become aware you were crying. But you were also smiling. You put everything you had in you into that smile. Then she smiled too. She asked you: 'Where'd you get that hair, girl?' You both laughed, your bodies shaking in pain, in spasm, in dread. You blew her kisses and said: 'My dear, my dear.' Her arms began to stretch out again, parting the air, rent by the monotonous sounds of the apparatus attached to the bodies of the old men in the other beds. She didn't say anything else. The darkness in her eyes had been exchanged for an instant by warmth. By something that looked like calm. Maybe she could see in your eyes that she was still alive.

She died a few days later. You didn't need anyone to tell you. You knew. You felt her pass through your hospital room, weightless and smiling. A sparkling silver light shimmered around her. Her hair was long and thick. There was no fear in her eyes. You thought then that a world in which God exists was possible.

It's Tuesday evening. They're preparing you for the operation. They shave you and give you an enema. You don't feel anything. Your body is accustomed to doing all those things it doesn't want to do. You tell yourself again that all will be well. The doctor, the gynaecologist who will do the operation, has a calm, gentle, comforting voice. She too tells you all will be well. You believe her.

When she leaves your room, your fear returns. Your fear is black and trembling. It looks like a pudding with too much sugar, sticky. It's a black hole opening up and you're falling into it. A greedy mouth of nothingness that devours all in its path. Tar on the road that sticks to your soles. Icy air that scours your skin. The distorted image of a broken mirror.

They give you a tranquillizer, but you can't sleep. Around midnight the anaesthetist, a man who's been caring for you for a month now, comes, taking on your fears of all that could go wrong. He decides they shouldn't wait until morning but give you a transfusion now. They attach a bag of thick, red, stranger's blood to a vein. As soon as it starts, you feel a heavy, unpleasant taste in your mouth, in your throat. As though you were eating someone's body.

It's all right, you tell yourself, *it's all right. This will help you. Don't think about the fact that a stranger is pouring into you.*

After half an hour you start shaking. You jump off the bed. Elvira, the nurse spending the night with you, brings a pile of blankets and covers you. The transfusion is turned off. Your body has rejected it. The anaesthetist is beside your bed. He can't hide his anxiety.

It's three in the morning when you calm down a bit, when that cold that had seemed to be gnawing your bones leaves you. Elvira asks whether you know any suras to recite. You say you don't. You cry. For the next half hour, or hour, or two hours, you don't know any more, she stands beside you and strokes your hair while her lips quietly recite prayers, barely audibly. You're quite certain this is the end of you.

You don't know what happens the following morning in the hospital wards, the corridors, among all those doctors endeavouring to get your body's consent to recover. They come and say they can't operate. They must find a way of getting your levels right. They send you home. You say nothing. You don't ask whether they're sending you home to die because they can't help you. Your voice is unable to get out of your throat, through your lips.

Later, you're in your son's room. You lie beside him. You hug him. You stay like that for hours, you and that child to whom you're not in a position to say anything, to explain anything. The darkness begins slowly to disperse. Your breath comes evenly. Time has a beginning and an end. Space has firmer edges. Your child is a fishing line that draws you out of the turbulent sea of panic, a pillar to which you cling, pulled out of the current carrying you beyond return.

On Tuesday, you go back to hospital. You're nourished by the bodies of your children through those nights, the three of you packed into one bed, those days you don't take your hands from them. As you hear their steady breathing in their sleep, the night opens and the fear falls away from you. You feel only total love. You know that, if there is a God, He is here. You know your time has not yet come. You have never been more present in yourself. The world has never made so much sense. You too are pure love, there's nothing apart from love. You send it to Aida. Her hair is silver, her face is calm. You understand each other perfectly in this farewell. You're removed from yourself. Completely aware that death is only the death of the body. Its surrender. Your body isn't ready to give up yet.

They don't know what happened to your blood during those few days you spent at home. The change is miraculous. 'As though you're a different person,' says the anaesthetist, happy at last. The operation is scheduled again, for the following day. They shave you and give you an enema again. They give you a tranquillizer. This time you sleep.

In the morning, your body is once again an object, exposed to a multitude of busy hands. You don't resist. You know all will be well. They prepare you in the operating theatre. The anaesthetist is above your head. His face is anxious, vigilant, concentrated. Your life is in his hands. You'll fall asleep quickly, into a sleep that will enable the operation, which will go perfectly. Before you fall asleep, you look at him and say, 'You know that moment when Charlie Brown says to Snoopy: "We'll all die one day,

Snoopy!" And Snoopy replies: "True, but all the other days we won't."'

He looks at you in disbelief. His expression begins to change. You've already fallen asleep, but you're quite certain he's laughing.

List of the parts of the body you have lost between you:

Dad:
    Two metres of intestine
    Left toe
    Right leg

Mum:
    Left breast
    Womb and ovaries
    Spleen

You:
    Right breast
    Left breast
    Womb and ovaries

(You deliberately divide your breasts into two parts. So your list isn't shorter than theirs. To draw that cosmic line of loss. To insure the remainder of your body.)

Your brother is thirty-eight and has a complete body.

You're twenty-six. Your daughter will soon be a year old. You live in your family house, on the first floor, in a separate apartment. Your parents are below you, on the ground floor. For the last two years, Dad hasn't had a right leg. That's just another involuntary suicide that went wrong. He's in a wheelchair. You have to consider him. Help him with all the things he can't do himself.

You're in the kitchen. It's 10 June 1999. You're making a puree for your daughter. You're holding the little bottle in your left hand. You pour hazelnut chocolate flakes into it. You add warm milk. Suddenly, as though the world around you begins to disintegrate, you notice a hole in reality, a double stitch, an instant when things leave their path. Your hand drops the bottle. Your fingers just open. The thick mixture of chocolate mush and liquid milk spills over the kitchen. Over the floor, the rug, the cupboards, even the ceiling. Like a volcano you didn't know was there. Before you can pull yourself together, the telephone rings. It's your mother.

He's not well. You sit beside him again while you wait for the ambulance. Again the smell is heavy and suffocating. This time he can't keep his eyes on you. The pain is too strong. His body jerks in a spasm, in a strange dance, a hidden implosion. You know something is bursting inside him. Something potent and tough is fragmenting to finally make an end. There are words you want to say, but your lips are firmly closed. Your hand searches again for his. He can't feel it. You think he's already left you, that there's nothing here apart from the jerking body.

The next day, in the hospital, they open his stomach. The pain comes from there. Alarmed by what they see (what kind of abyss have they looked into?), they sew him up as fast as possible. He wakes in still greater pain. His frail, broken body throws one leg out of the bed. He tries to stand, unconscious, distraught, tries to run away from everything, from his own self. They tie his arms and leg down with thick belts. The spasms don't stop until deep into the night, which he meets alone. Death is proclaimed at 01.35. You don't know who's standing beside his bed to confirm the end. You don't know whether a single hand reaches for his to console him with a touch an instant before everything is finally lost.

Before you've even mourned him, a new illness moves into your lives. Just two weeks later your mother is diagnosed with breast cancer. The circles you're all passing through are the links in a chain in which there's nothing but illness. You know that now.

Your recovery from the fourth operation takes a long time. Weeks. Your body is accustomed to pain. Your bed is big and empty. In the centre is your body, stretched out, longing for a touch. For Grandad's hand holding your foot. For a lover stronger than fear while the heat of his body warms the quivering air under your duvet. For a man who will love you utterly, you in your fragmentariness, in your shattered body. You, a woman who rejects the attributes of a woman. A darkness of blood never capable of finding peace. And passing his fingers over your body presses all the dread out of it. Sometimes you jerk out of sleep and feel that he's already here, in the room, above the bed. He has the eyes of a wolf and watches you until your sight grows used to the dark.

You wake sweating. What's flaring in you is a sudden summer fire, an onslaught of heat, and for a moment your consciousness clouds over. The gynaecologist said you won't naturally enter the menopause for another fifteen years. Such is the hyperproduction of oestrogen in your body. You're what's called oestrogen dominant. You think maybe that's the reason. Perhaps you've sensed that the world has no place for such a woman, hence this shameful betrayal, this rejection of parts of yourself, the feeling there is always too much of you, that you have to cut bits off in order to belong, to fit in.

Your temperature won't go down. Your breast is increasingly big and red. You're increasingly tired. Nothing exists apart from weariness and the papers on which is written information about the processes in your body. You're obsessed with CRP, the indicator of inflammation in the organism. Since the operation it's been better, but it's still not within normal limits. It's clear the breast is inflamed.

You pack the same suitcase that is already accustomed to the Mostar–Zagreb journey. You go to the surgeon who operated on you twice and at least three more times refilled your right boob, with a physiological solution, with a big needle, through a valve under your skin which resembled a hidden earpiece. He's undecided. He doesn't know what should be done, whether to take it all out or wait. He tells you to decide. That decision isn't one that ought to belong to you, that's all you know.

You set off alone into the battle against an inflammation whose cause you don't know. You take turmeric tablets. Oregano oil. Your breast is constantly covered with frozen cabbage leaves. You try to draw the fire out of it, to guess what still refuses to accept the shape of a woman, what still wants to be cut out, broken off. Still unaware of how much you are a woman, a complete woman, perfect and beautiful regardless of the shape of your body.

You try to fill your day with something other than changing dressings and cooking dinner. You don't succeed. You're worn out. However much you sleep, it isn't enough. That bed from which you fled for a year is the only place you want to be.

You keep going until March, when you finally realize you can't take any more. Your right boob is enormous. Red. With no nipple. As though something unknown and large-headed wants to break away from you. You take that same suitcase out of the cupboard. Once again you face the grey, drawn-out road to Zagreb, to that city that's really become your hospital.

You look for a different doctor. One who will know what has to be done. You realize it will mean another operation. You must decide whether you'll now finally, this time definitively, part from your right boob. From this bulging shape on your body pretending to be a boob. Will you say that they should take it all away? Including the skin under which sometime later another prosthesis could be inserted? That's done when there's inflammation or infection. The prosthesis is removed, the skin left, and three to six months later a new one is put in. Those are two operations. Or one, if you no longer want your false boob.

You delve into yourself, crawl into your darkness, to discover why you need that boob so badly. Why won't you accept life without it? Is it important, at the end of the day? Shouldn't you be indifferent by now? You know you're not. Maybe because then they'll have won. They – that invisible and unknown something that's conspired against you. The chasm that wants to swallow you. All those faces that death changes into, to deceive you. You won't let anyone win apart from yourself. You're stronger than anything. Than pain. Than all the deaths. You'll fill yourself with silicone, that plastic, feel that it's an organic part of yourself. Not accept that the illness decides how your body will look. Nothing can break your strength. However often they knock you down, you'll get up again. Strike out with everything you have in you. Paying no attention to pain. *Under your pressure I only grow stronger*, you tell death. It still smells of jasmine, it's not succeeding in hiding its tracks.

The new surgeon says it can all be done at once. And must be done immediately.

It's Monday. You get into the car and go home. On Tuesday you have tests. Your blood is on the borderline of what's acceptable for the operation. On Wednesday you go back to Zagreb. They operate on Thursday. This time, the cuts are under the breast. The prostheses are removed and replaced with new ones. The pain is the same as after the second operation. Your recovery also. You know it all. You've already been through it all. You don't think about anything. You don't ask why. You've never wondered about that. You're clever enough to know there's no answer to that question, that it can only drain your strength.

For the next four weeks, day and night, you again wear a large uncomfortable bra which looks like a waistcoat and keeps your breasts motionless. You've learned how to raise yourself into a sitting position, with the least possible pain. You push another pillow under your head. You bend your legs at the knees. With your feet and elbows you shift, slowly, centimetre by centimetre, from left to right, from right to left, upwards. You straighten up as much as you can, in one minimal forward movement. Under your skin you feel the shifting of those insertions, as though they are sliding downwards, as though they're going to slither down you, slicing into your tissue. Pain can't get to you any more. You don't resist it. You let it do what it has to. It's temporary, you are eternal.

Mostly, you just keep quiet. There's no room in your mouth for words. They're superfluous. That too is one of your deaths. Now comes life.

You're sitting on your bed. Other objects have vanished, the night sky is all there is around you. The blackness preserves glimmers of blue. The stars are blazing sunflowers. They are recovering from dizziness, finally at rest. Meteors float about. The denial of the dimension of time liberates them from the fate of speed. Shooting stars have fallen over your bed, like cats which have come to warm you with their bodies.

The first to come in is Aida. Her skin glows in the darkness. In her eyes, like two wooden boats, are anchored the past and the future. Her smile is drowsy, soothing. It's the smile of those for whom no secret exists. She sits down on the floor beside the bed. Her smile tells you that she has brought all the others with her.

You hear a rustling of brocade, as though a flock of bats is flying towards you. A river of red dresses settles round you.

Medea's eyes aren't salty. Medusa's snakes have come to life. The scars on the Amazons' exposed chests are silver threads woven by the goddess of the Moon. The women with black holes in their mouths now have crystal teeth. Laughter bounces off them, sprinkles you. They take off their dresses, which become red clouds on which they stand. Their bodies are naked, their hair loose. They take each other's hands. They dance. They twist their bodies. From a heavenly gramophone pours Bowie's 'Wild is the Wind'. Cosmic drums play. Their bodies are in a trance.

> … You're spring to me, all things to me
> Don't you know, you're life itself …

Above you all the Moon revolves like a disco ball.

We've grown tired of death, they say. *Now we're going to live through your body.*

Slowly, one by one, they enter you. Skin sinks into skin, flesh swallows flesh, bones mesh together. You are each of them. A thousand lives are booming within you. *You are life itself.*

They inform you that it was a hospital infection. Your body had become infected during one of the earlier operations. It's impossible to know when. That detail is inconsequential.

A few days after the operation, you feel much better. As though someone had switched on a light in the entrance hall of your childhood. Everything is clear and easy. Your blood is improving. The new breasts are full and lovely. You don't admit to anyone that you feel they don't belong to you, that they've been hooked onto you, aren't an integral part. At every movement you feel an inertia that pushes them in the opposite direction. That doesn't bother you. You're used to it. The right one still has its eye closed. You don't want to have the nipple reconstructed. Instead, you get a tattoo. A mandala the size and colour of your left nipple. You restore your body's symmetry. That body can be loved. You've chosen it. It's still the body of a woman, through all your transformations. Enchanting, beautiful and soft, self-contained. The body of a warrior. Perfectly sculpted through all your defeats, and your victories. The scars scrawled on it are the map of your journey. The truest story about you, which words cannot grasp.

It's summer 2016. You wake up early. You go for a walk. Faster each day. Your body cuts through the air. Six kilometres, at a speed of six kilometres an hour. That's your optimal speed. You restore movement to your body. You repeat to yourself: *The body is movement. Movement is life.* In this body, you're now healthy. Nothing can stop you any more.

Your world is freed of questions. In the darkness inside you, the crying has stopped. Somewhere along the way, the child in you, the little girl who feels only pain, has found peace. The woman in you is ready to be loved, in this body which itself chooses its shape, overcoming the borders that endeavour to reduce its perfection. Your lover has gone. Nor does M come back to you any more. That's all right. You've perfected the skill of losing. You've learned to let pain pass through you as through a sieve. Perhaps you still hope that in one of your nights those wolf's eyes will come to life, and, after all the deaths, you will find love.

There is just one place left to which you must return.

You get into the car. You drive to the coast. To that village on the Pelješac peninsula which is your true home. Pebbles crunch under your feet. Vineyards stretch out around you. You climb up a steep path to the chapel on the cliff. On the hill opposite, withstanding the years, is your tree. That's enough of a sign. There's a stone wall behind you. By now the bottle of water you're holding is hot. You take a warm sip. You close your eyes. Below, the sea dazzles, a blueness capable of singing. In the distance are islands, like the remnants of the clay from which the gods formed the earth.

THE PEIRENE SUBSCRIPTION

Since 2011, Peirene Press has run a subscription service which has brought a world of translated literature to thousands of readers. We seek out great stories and original writing from across the globe, and work with the best translators to bring these books into English – before sending each one to our subscribers, six to eight weeks ahead of publication. All of our novellas are beautifully designed collectible paperback editions, printed in the UK using sustainable materials.

Join our reading community today and subscribe to receive three translated novellas a year, as well as invitations to events and launch parties and discounts on all our titles. We also offer a gift subscription, so you can share your literary discoveries with friends and family.

A one-year subscription costs £35, including UK shipping. International postage costs apply.

www.peirenepress.com/subscribe

'The foreign literature specialist'

The Sunday Times

'A class act'

The Guardian

PEIRENE | STEVNS
TRANSLATION PRIZE

The Peirene Stevns Translation Prize was launched in 2018 to support up-and-coming translators.

Open to all translators without a published novel, this prize looks to award great translation and to offer new ways of entry into the world of professional translation.

The winner receives a £3,500 commission to translate a text selected by Peirene Press, the opportunity to spend two months at a retreat in the Pyrenees and a dedicated one-on-one mentorship throughout the translation process.

The Peirene Stevns Prize focuses on a different language each year and opens to submissions from October to January.

With thanks to Martha Stevns, without whom this prize would not be possible.